RISPONDIMI

RISPONDIMI

SUSANNA TAMARO

*Translated from the Italian
by John Cullen*

NAN A. TALESE

DOUBLEDAY

New York   London   Toronto   Sydney   Auckland

PUBLISHED BY NAN A. TALESE
an imprint of Doubleday
a division of Random House, Inc.
1540 Broadway, New York, New York 10036

DOUBLEDAY is a trademark of Doubleday
a division of Random House, Inc.

First published in Italy by Rizzoli

This book is a work of fiction. Names, characters,
businesses, organizations, places, events, and incidents either
are the product of the author's imagination or are used fictitiously.
Any resemblance to actual persons, living or dead, events,
or locales is entirely coincidental.

Library of Congress Cataloging-in-Publication Data

Tamaro, Susanna, 1957–
[Rispondimi. English]
Rispondimi / Susanna Tamaro ; translated from the Italian
by John Cullen.—1. ed.
p.   cm.
I. Cullen, John, 1942–   II. Title.
PQ4880.A445 R5713   2002
853'.914—dc21   2001044290

ISBN 0-385-50351-2
Copyright © 2001 by Limmat Stiftung
English language translation © 2001 by John Cullen
All Rights Reserved
PRINTED IN THE UNITED STATES OF AMERICA
April 2002
First Edition in the United States of America

CONTENTS

Remain in my love.
—JOHN 15:9

RISPONDIMI

ONE

I N FACT, it was just this past Christmas, the last holidays I spent at my aunt and uncle's. The weather was cold, and fog blanketed the village. Life there was as boring as always, nobody ever called, nobody came to see me. My uncle fell asleep watching the dancers on television, my aunt crocheted huge bedspreads. The plastic tree blinked in the semidarkness like a broken traffic light.

Even at midday, fog lay over the house like a shroud. Every half hour I looked out the window to see if the sun had broken through. You could never see a thing. At night I dreamed I had long, long arms, so long that I could reach the sky. I reached up there and grabbed the clouds and pushed them aside, one after the other, as though they were curtains in a movie theater. I started to get angry. Does the sun really exist? I wondered. At last I found it, its bright ray struck me in the middle of my forehead. It struck me and no one else, because I had been the one looking for it, I had flushed it out with my enormous arms, with the force of my will.

On New Year's Eve I went into the woodshed and got drunk. At intervals, the sounds of passing cars reached me from outside. Everyone was in motion, hurtling through the fog. Going where? Going to kill themselves, perhaps, out of pure sadness, even before they ate the big New Year's Eve dinner. The wood smelled moldy. It looked wet and glossy, like the wood of a sunken galleon. Everything was whirling around me, and I thought, I'm in the belly of the whale. It's swallowed me, and I'll never be able to escape. I'm a prisoner in a castle dungeon, or maybe I'm already in the afterlife and this is my grave. The wood is rotting, and my bones have started rotting, too. If this is the grave, where's the next world? Eventually, a crack should open, the Light should come in somewhere. Or flames should blaze up.

Was I supposed to believe this? To fall back into the trap and keep on believing?

All the same, my mother had to be somewhere. Maybe she'd gone to hell, and that's why I couldn't see her. Or maybe there wasn't anything, maybe there was nothing at all. After a year, you were worms, and after two, dust.

"Say a little prayer for your mama and for the souls in purgatory." When I was in boarding school, that's what the nuns told me every night. I obeyed them; I knelt there with my hands joined and raised my eyes heavenward. I expected my mother to appear at any moment, a sudden flash of light followed by wind. I would recognize her by the heat, by the little tornado of warmth that would rise up from the pit of my stomach. Love, I'd tell myself, has brought her back from the land of the dead.

I prayed and prayed, but the only thing that flashed, on and off, was a defective light bulb.

Did love really exist? And if it did, what form did it assume?

The more time passed, the less I was able to understand. Love was a word, a word like table, window, lamp. Or was it something else? How many kinds of love were there?

I had believed in it since I was a little girl, the way you believe that there are elves who live inside trees. One day, however, I looked into the cracks in some tree trunks, under the caps of the mushrooms. There weren't any elves, nor any fairies, either; only moss, lichen, a little mold, and a few insects.

Instead of embracing, the insects were devouring one another.

My mother died when I was almost eight years old. An automobile accident while I was at school. I remember that day clearly. The teacher brought me into the principal's office. One of them kept her arm around my shoulder, the other one moved her mouth: "Something terrible has happened. . . ."

I stood there, very still, without crying. I thought, I wonder if I'll ever find her smell again?

Why do faces disappear from memory as time passes, but not smells? What was her scent made of, what was in it? Cheap cologne, for sure, mixed with the smell of her skin and the fragrance of soap or talcum powder. My mother was constantly washing herself.

During my first seven years, we were always together. We lived in a small apartment. She was cheerful, flamboyant, brightly colored. At night, after she tucked me in, she went to work, and when I woke up there she was again, standing next to the bed. She'd announce, "Now arriving, a shower of kisses!" and throw herself on me, laughing.

That's how it was, and that's how I thought it would always be.

I didn't yet know that our names weren't carved in stone, but scribbled on a blackboard. Every so often someone made a pass with the eraser and another name vanished from the list. Did he wield the eraser precisely, purposefully? Did he wield it inadvertently? Was that the very name he wanted to erase, or was it maybe the one just above, or the one just below?

We had hung a small picture of Jesus over the door in the kitchenette. Below the picture, a tiny light was always on. Although it didn't burn your fingers, it moved like a little flame. Jesus was holding his heart in his hand, but that didn't bother me, because instead of being disheveled and screaming in pain, he had perfectly combed hair and rosy cheeks and he was smiling and didn't seem scared at all. "Who's that man?" I asked, the first time I saw him.

"He's a friend," Mama replied, "a friend who loves you."

"Does he love you, too?"

"Of course. He loves everybody."

For me, the smell of that day—the day she died—will always be the smell of freshly baked bread. A bag from a bakery was hanging on the back of the principal's chair. The fragrance had got out of the bag and permeated the whole room.

On the windowsill, a sweet potato was languishing in a glass of dirty water.

The "something terrible" was death.

"I want to see her," I said.

"I'm sorry. That's not possible."

In the succeeding days, an almost infinite number of smells overlaid hers. The smell of the hospital, an ugly smell that was new to me; the smell of turned earth and flowers that were already old when they arrived; the smells of her friends, Pina, Giulia, and Cinzia, who hugged me again and again; the smell of the cassock worn by the old priest, who was in a hurry and talking fast; the smell of a bologna sandwich that someone was eating nearby; the smell of the solid pine credenza that we had in the kitchen.

Now she had to stay closed up in that other credenza, the long, narrow one.

Her girl friends cried and blew their noses. The lady who'd brought me to the funeral held me tight, as if she were afraid I'd fly away to heaven.

"Am I supposed to cry, too?" I asked her. She moved her head back and forth, as if to say "Yes." I tried to do it, but with small success. I had only one thought in my head. Where does a person go when she's not anywhere anymore?

The next day I began to ask Jesus to make me go blind. I'd been told at school that he healed many sightless people by spitting on their eyelids. If he did that, I thought, he could do the opposite as well. They say that certain animals are capable of doing it, they spray a liquid into your eyes and you sink into the world of shadows.

That was what I wished for with all my might. To pass into the world where there was nothing to see anymore, neither streets nor houses nor cars nor faces nor morning nor afternoon. Only night. A night in the middle of the ocean, under an overcast sky, with no stars and no moon and no lighthouses on the horizon.

Ordinarily, blind people use their sense of touch to get around. I would be a different sort of blind person— I'd go around sniffing. I'd smell the red traffic light and the green traffic light, I'd know the smell of rain and the more intense smell that means it's going to snow. I'd use my sense of smell to recognize pleasant people, unpleasant people, people I could trust, and people who had to be bitten before they got too close.

I asked Jesus to bring me into the shadows because I was convinced that my mother was hiding in there somewhere. If I wandered up and down in the darkness, sooner or later I'd pick up a trace of her scent, and then that trace would lead me to her, to the stormy tumult of her kisses.

The smell of disinfectant, the smell of vegetable soup, onions, leeks, the smell of stale air, of dust, of dirty skirts, the smell of pee in the bed, of cheap soap, the smell of dampness, the smell of incense. On the chart of these smells, I didn't recognize a single one as my own.

There was a nun in the boarding school who was always putting her arms around me. She wanted to give me comfort, but all she did was frighten me.

Was that the way my life was going to smell now, the odor that I was going to have to get used to?

I wasn't blind yet, but all the same I had learned to do a trick with my eyes. Whenever I was face to face with someone, I imagined that I was a snail. I moved my eyes back and forth, back and forth, until everything became opaque.

The only time I was happy was at night, when we were all in pajamas next to our beds and Sister would say, "Let's fold our hands, girls, and say a little prayer to Jesus."

Jesus had followed me from one life to another, and since he was my friend and he loved me, that was a good thing. So, with my hands joined, I repeated a prayer in my mind: "Please, since you're my friend and Mama's too, make us be together again forever."

The Jesus of the dormitory, however, was different from the Jesus of the kitchenette. Instead of smiling and holding his heart in his hand, he was nailed to a cross, dirty, almost naked, with his eyes closed. There he hung in his pain, and he didn't look at anyone at all.

In the meantime, they were trying to find my relatives. I'd never had a father. Mama had neither brothers nor sisters. Her parents had died a long time ago.

One day, the girl whose bed was next to mine said, "You're lucky. You're going to wind up getting adopted."

So the weeks passed, and this too became a dream of mine. I didn't want another mama, but I would have liked to have a father, finally, and a house with a room of my own, with my own toys, my own smells.

One day a social worker arrived. She had red cheeks and an extremely threadbare bottle-green overcoat. "You're lucky!" she exclaimed merrily. "Today we're going to pack your bags, and tomorrow you go to your aunt and uncle's. Uncle Luciano is your grandfather's brother. He's married, but he has no children. From now on, you'll spend Christmas holidays and summers with them in the country. Are you happy?"

I said neither yes nor no. I stood still, with my snail's eyes moving back and forth.

The next morning, my uncle came to pick me up. His shoes squeaked when he crossed the big entrance hall. Instead of kissing me, he held out his hand: "I'm Luciano, pleased to meet you."

His car had red plastic seats, very shiny. In the back there were two round crocheted pillows covered with lace. They swayed like big jellyfish at every bend in the road. Neither of us spoke.

Shortly before we arrived at the farm, he said to me, "Now you'll meet your aunt Elide."

My aunt looked as though she'd been carved out of wood. She had hard, red cheeks and a very large nose. She gave me two kisses like bites and said, "Welcome."

That afternoon I helped her clean the henhouse. The next day, we made the Christmas cookies. She didn't say much. "Pass me that; take this."

I was given a room upstairs, with a big, cold bed. There was a small table, a wardrobe, and a tile floor. From my window I could see the overpass on the provincial highway. The cars went *voom, voom,* and the trucks went *grrrrn.*

It was often foggy. On those days, the big tractor-trailers seemed like mammoths. They emerged out of the void, like ghosts, and then the void swallowed them up again.

That Christmas, under the little plastic tree with the flashing lights, I found a package. Inside the package, there was a box. Inside the box, there was a white blouse.

"Do you like it?" Aunt Elide asked me.

"Yes," I answered.

Actually, the white blouse meant nothing to me. The only thing I really would have liked was a teddy bear to share my bed with. The one I'd always had was gone.

It had wound up in the land of shadows, like every-thing else.

That Christmas I got a white blouse, and I got a white blouse almost every Christmas after that. A blouse that was always more severe, always more chaste than the last one.

TWO

I N BOARDING SCHOOL, I spent all my time alone. Every now and then, one of the nuns would take me aside and say, "It's not good to cut yourself off, it'll just make you sad." Then, to appease her, I'd rejoin the other girls and take my place in the circle, but nobody ever sent the ball my way. I'd stay there for a while, but then I'd withdraw again and sit on a bench, alone with my thoughts.

According to what the nuns repeatedly told us, there are good thoughts and bad thoughts. Which thoughts were good, and which thoughts were bad? How was it possible to distinguish them? Thoughts have no scent, and that makes everything more difficult.

I walked along the little paths in the garden, thinking. If God were really kind, he would have given a smell to thoughts, too, so that it would be possible to distinguish them as soon as they form in the mind. Getting close to a rose is one thing, getting close to a primrose is something else. The first one stuns you with its fragrance; you hardly notice the other. In the same way, bad thoughts ought to stink—like shit or rotten fish, for example— while good ones should have a warm, soft aroma like chocolate or vanilla. That would make the world a simpler place. Nobody would be able to hide behind words, because everyone would be able to notice the sweet fragrance or the awful stench. Anyone with bad thoughts or evil intentions would be found out even before he opened his mouth.

In catechism class, back when I was around eight years old, I discovered the existence of my guardian angel. From that day on, whenever anyone asked me, "Why are you always alone?" I'd reply, "I'm not alone, I've got my angel with me."

"Rosa's angel is always with her," the nuns would whisper, watching me from a distance. "God bless you," the old nun who was the doorkeeper would murmur as she passed me. And so I was able to think in peace.

There was something that had been tormenting me for some time. It had to do with Jesus. I'd done a little figuring. There were twelve of us in my dormitory room, and every night we all asked him for something. There were four other dorm rooms, all with a similar number of requests, and then there were the nuns. All told, just in that one place, he had quite a few people to take care of. And if he went outside the boarding school, the number increased frighteningly. How did Jesus manage to remember all those requests, and more importantly, how did he fulfill them? Then again, were we really sure that he'd fulfill them? Mama used to tell me that Jesus loved me, and that he loved her, too. The nuns said that he loved everybody.

But what was love? I couldn't understand it. It wasn't a smell, nor a coin you could buy things with. The nuns spoke about love as though it were the glue that held the world together, but they covered up our windows and read our letters out of fear that love would burst out. What love were they talking about?

The more I pondered, the less I understood. I asked the girl who sat next to me. "It's when a man and a woman sleep naked, one on top and the other on the bottom."

The summers I spent with my uncle and aunt were interminable. No one ever came for a visit. Except for the August holiday, when we went to a nearby sanctuary dedicated to the Virgin Mary, we never took any trips. The air was motionless, the light was blinding, the heat brought various forms of excrement—rabbit pee, chicken shit—to fermentation. If you wanted to go for a walk, you had to hold your nose.

"You'd better get used to it, little miss," my aunt said nastily. One day the henhouse, the rabbit hutch, the woodshed, and the house and garden would be mine. That's what my aunt was talking about. I had to get used to the place because one day all this would be my life: cleaning chickens, wringing chicken necks, picking tomatoes, peeling them, stewing them, skinning rabbits, and then in the evenings sitting exhausted in front of the house to watch the big trucks on the highway flash by.

"If it hadn't been for us . . ." She said that a lot.

If it hadn't been for you, I went on to myself, I'd have a nice house and a daddy by now. Or maybe I'd be by the seaside, at summer camp with the nuns. Wherever I'd be would be better than staying here, inhaling engine exhaust and the methane of decomposition.

People had more smell during the summer, too. At a hundred feet, with my eyes closed, I could have scented the difference between my aunt and my uncle, between the priest and the postman.

In the heat, the noises became terrible. *Vrooom, vrooom:* trucks revving on the overpass. *Bzzz, bzzz:* flies buzzing. *Krrro-ahk, krrro-ahk:* frogs croaking in a nearby ditch. And at night, the mosquitoes. Mosquitoes of every size. As soon as you turned out the light, they were at you, zooming around your ears, *zss, zss.* Killing them was useless. For every dead one, ten more came out of nowhere.

My aunt had bought a sort of lamp at a fair and put it in the kitchen. Any insect that grazed that lamp got carbonized. The sound was *cheesh*, the smell was like burned chicken. At every demise, my aunt shouted, "Got him!" and then announced the new tally for the day.

Zss, krrro-ahk, vrooom, cheesh, bzz-bzz . . . who could I talk to? During the summer, the questions that had accumulated in my head during the winter turned into a hat that was too tight for me.

My aunt wasn't fond of me, my uncle was indifferent. The postman always gave me a caramel, and the priest couldn't stand me.

I knew it the first time I saw him. He smelled like soup, like a cellar, like something that was somehow dirty. He had narrow little eyes like a wild boar. When my aunt presented me to him, he stood there unmoving and looked at me as though he were eyeing an insect. He didn't hold out his hand to me or caress me. He just touched his nose and said, "Ah, yes, Marisa's daughter."

All the same, one day I went to see him. If Father Firmato wasn't able to answer me, who on earth could? He was sitting in the back of the church, taking a nap in the cool shade. I sat down next to him and touched his sleeve.

"It's you," he mumbled.

"There's something I want to know."

"Tell me."

"What is love?"

He turned to look at me. His eyes were watery and slow.

"How old are you?"

"Twelve."

"Love is sin."

Of all the sins, Father Firmato preferred those of the flesh, which was the reason why the other children called him "Father Beefsteak" behind his back. Every Sunday, after going off on more or less lengthy tangents, he always wound up talking about his favorite topic:

perdition through the senses. In Don Firmato's view, an insuperable wall divided the world into two parts. Some people were on one side of the wall, some were on the other. One side was hell, the other was heaven, and your place was predetermined before you were born. There was no possibility of choice. Everything was decided from the beginning.

One night, someone wrote "Firmato = Filthy" in red paint on the rectory wall. When I passed and saw it, I laughed before I could stop myself.

That very afternoon, the carabinieri arrived and asked my aunt a lot of questions. Was the door of the house unlocked at night, or wasn't it? Was it possible to sneak out and come back in through the windows without anyone noticing? Then they went up to my room and looked in the wardrobe and under the bed. They checked my hands and my forearms. They even examined my fingernails to see whether any traces of paint had remained.

"My niece is a good girl," my aunt said, speaking to their backs. "She goes to mass with me every Sunday. She goes to bed early at night. And besides, Sergeant, if she had done it, I would have killed her with my own hands."

The carabinieri nodded, their faces grave. Father Firmato must have been positive that I was the culprit. As far as he was concerned, I should have been burning in the flames of hell already. My aunt defended me solely because she knew it was impossible for me to leave the house at night. Every evening, in fact, she locked all the doors, and you couldn't get down from the third floor, where I slept, without hurting yourself.

Nevertheless, the next day I had to join the little group of the faithful who were charged with obliterating the writing on the rectory wall. When the priest passed close to me, he hissed, "Like mother, like daughter. She's in hell, and you're already in the waiting room."

My mother was a whore. When I was eight, I didn't yet know this, I was convinced that she worked at night cleaning offices. I kept on believing that until I was eleven.

In the meanwhile, the dream of following her among the shadows had disappeared. The nuns had called in a psychologist to help me. The psychologist came to the boarding school. We talked, just the two of us, in one of the rooms.

"She's dead," he said to me. "Can you understand what that means? It means that your mama doesn't walk on the earth anymore, that you'll never open a door and see her anymore. You won't be able to touch her or hug her ever again. You have to get used to living with just your beautiful memories of her." Then he barely touched me and went on, "If you want to cry, go ahead."

Everybody wanted me to cry, but I didn't feel like it. Instead of crying, I considered a question: where does garbage go? Because garbage is the same way. One day the plastic bag's inside the house, in the corner under the sink, and the next day it's not there anymore. A big truck comes and swallows it up. Once the truck has passed, all that remains is a bad smell.

Death couldn't be very different, it went around swallowing up people like so many garbage bags, leaving behind nothing but a cloud of bad odor. The same odor as when the tractor-trailers on the provincial highway ran over a dog.

I learned the truth from Aunt Elide, who screamed it in my face one morning. She was angry with me for some reason. At such times her eyes became glass and her tongue metal. "It's time to put an end to this farce," she yelled. Then she told me the truth, bead by bead, like a rosary. "Your mother didn't die in a wreck. She got run over while she was waiting for customers at a bend in the ring road."

"What was she selling?" I asked.

My aunt gave me a skeptical look. "You don't understand? She was selling her body. She was a woman who knew how to do only one thing: open her legs."

From that day on, every time she spoke about her, that's what Aunt Elide called her. The woman who opened her legs.

I put up with it for more than a year. Then, one morning when we were in the kitchen, as soon as she started to say, "The only thing she knew how to do . . ." I lost my temper.

"She knew how to open her arms, too!" I screamed at her.

My aunt became very pale.

"You little wretch," she hissed. "To think of the sacrifices we make for you!"

I grabbed the tongs and took a piece of burning wood from the fireplace and waved it around near the curtains.

"Touch me and I'll set the whole place on fire."

My uncle came to her aid. "Water puts out fire," he said, and threw the contents of a pitcher in my face.

Was that the day when I began to hate them?

I believe it was.

I was in my room, writing them little notes. I hate you, I hope you die, I hope you get hit by a car, have a stroke, catch some awful disease. I made some drawings to go with the words, then I tore everything into tiny pieces, went into the bathroom, and relieved myself all over them.

In the presence of my aunt and uncle I pretended nothing was wrong, I tried hard to be nice. I was afraid of reprisals. My uncle was always threatening to lock me in the woodshed, because it was full of mice, spiders, and snakes. To overcome my fear, I started going in there on my own. No one ever found me there, no one bothered me. Before long, the woodshed had become my favorite refuge. I was more afraid of human beings than of mice and snakes.

Once, when I was riding my aunt's bicycle along a white road, I came across a woman with two children. She was hollering like a madwoman because there was a grass snake a few yards from her. I got off the bike, and to show her that the snake wouldn't hurt her I grabbed it by the tail and held it under her nose. "You see," I told her. "All you have to do is pick it up by the tail. There's no way it can curl itself up." Instead of thanking me, she kept on hollering like someone possessed.

The next day, the whole village was saying that there must be something wrong with me because I went around with snakes in my pocket and petted them on the head, the way you pet dogs.

THREE

B Y T H E T I M E I was thirteen, I was more than
tired of my aunt and uncle. Just imagining their
voices and their faces would send me into a state of
profound uneasiness. Therefore, a few days before
Christmas, I decided that I wouldn't go to their farm
that year. I asked for an appointment with the principal
and told her so.

"Why?" she asked me, looking me straight in
the eyes.

"Because I don't feel like it."

"Is there something wrong?"

"No, nothing. They're old and I get bored. That's
all."

"In that case I'm sorry, but you have to go to them.
The court put you in their custody. Besides, being alone
on Christmas Day is different from being alone on any
other day of the year. If you were to stay here, you'd end
up regretting it."

All night long I brooded over the idea of running
away, but in the morning I did the same identical thing I

had done in previous years. I caught a bus and went to the farm.

The cookies were already in the oven.

"You're here at last!" my aunt shouted when she saw me come in. "Change your clothes and clean the rabbits. Then come over here, we have to pluck the capon."

I spent the whole day before Christmas Eve working for her.

That evening, a thin, icy drizzle began to fall. We ate in silence, seated at the Formica table in the kitchen with the television on. The windowpanes were covered with steam. The turkey was boiling in a large pot. The bird was too big, so the stumps of its legs stuck out over the rim of the pot.

I washed the dishes and went to bed. The sheets were freezing, and the quilt seemed to be wet. *Voom grrrrn voom*. The noise of the cars came through the closed window. I felt sad, with that quiet sadness that comes before tears. From force of habit, a prayer sprang to my lips, but I drove it back down. I had outgrown teddy bears, and now I couldn't cling to prayers anymore. Then what was the antidote to sadness? I wanted to cry, but nothing came out of my eyes. My body felt as though it belonged to someone else. I tried to hug myself. Cold on cold. An embrace between two snakes, between two pieces of scrap metal. Now I'm going to jump out the window, I thought. I probably won't die, but at least I'll break my legs or my backbone, I'll spend Christmas in the hospital and the rest of my days in a wheelchair. At that precise moment, it seemed to me as though I smelled my mother's scent. I turned on the light. There was no one in the room. Where was it coming from? Was it really there, or had I just dreamed it? On the ceiling, above the bed, a mildew stain had appeared. It looked like a bear's snout, or the face of a monkey with his mouth open.

The sound of the television set was still rising from downstairs. The two monoliths were down there, sitting in armchairs covered with dust-repellent cellophane. Two dried-out insects. Two wizened mummies. My aunt commanded, and my uncle obeyed. "Yes, Elide. Fine, Elide. You're right, Elide."

All Christmas Eve, I tried to keep quiet. If my aunt gave an order, I carried it out at once. I did everything with my eyes lowered, because I didn't want them to be able to read my thoughts. Every now and then I went to my room, grabbed my pillow, and flung it against the wall as hard as I could; then I buried my face in it and screamed in silence.

That night we would open the presents, exchange kisses of gratitude, and gobble up cold turkey while watching a variety show on TV. My uncle would laugh at the most idiotic, the coarsest jokes.

I was expecting my sixth white blouse, but to my surprise I got a pair of blue wool gloves reinforced with imitation leather. I too surprised my aunt and uncle. Instead of the usual little vase made with my own hands or a pair of crocheted pot holders, I gave them a pear and an apple wrapped up in a pretty red ribbon. For years, when we were opening the presents, my aunt would sigh and say, "How lovely Christmas used to be when the only gifts were a couple of walnuts and an orange!" So I gave her what she wanted.

Then we sat down at the table. Just as my aunt was complaining that the *tortelloni* hadn't turned out as well as last year's and my uncle was reassuring her, saying that he thought they were probably even better, someone rang the doorbell. My aunt stretched out her neck like a turkey.

"Who can that be at this hour? And tonight of all nights?"

I got up and went to open the door. It was a Negro with a large bag. He was selling underwear and towels. The whites of his eyes shone in the night.

"You want to buy pretty things?" he asked me.

"Come in," I said. "We're having Christmas dinner."

My aunt leaped to her feet at once. "Who is it?" she shouted. "What's got into you? Why have you let him in?"

"Are we having Christmas dinner or not?" I replied.

"*We* are, but not him. If he was a Christian, he certainly wouldn't have picked this evening to go around selling his rags."

My uncle got to his feet and lightly touched the Negro's hand with his own.

"Thank you," he said, demonstrating his manly authority, "but we don't need anything." Then he accompanied him to the door.

When my uncle came back, my aunt asked him, "You made sure the door was locked?"

"Of course."

We started eating again in silence. On the television screen, children of all colors, got up like circus monkeys, were singing some inane Christmas songs while adults with glistening eyes stood around them and clapped their hands.

I banged my spoon against the rim of my plate.

The two monoliths raised their eyes.

"What if it had been Jesus?" I asked.

My aunt got up to gather the plates. "Don't talk non-sense. Jesus wasn't a Negro. And besides, he didn't go around selling underwear."

When the dish with the slices of boiled turkey was passed to me, I thought, they look like pieces of a corpse. In fact, they are pieces of a corpse. I left them untouched.

"How do you know you don't like it if you don't even taste it?"

Instead of telling her to go to hell, I merely said, "I'm not hungry anymore."

She stabbed a slice with her fork and slammed the turkey onto my plate. "Eat it anyway."

At that point, something strange happened. I felt my heart beginning to swell up. It seemed as though they had unscrewed an artery and attached a bicycle pump in its place. The gauge climbed, and my heart became wider. What would happen if it started beating against the sharp ends of my ribs?

So I opened my mouth.

"Why don't we talk about love?"

Right away Turkey Neck asked, "What sort of love?"

"I don't know. I'm asking the two of you. How many

kinds of love are there? Two? Three? Four? Ten? A thousand? Since you're married, you must know one kind at least, right? That's why people get married, isn't it? Or did you . . ."

My uncle rose to his feet, trembling all over.

"If you don't show some respect, I'll . . . !"

"I only asked a question! I don't know what love is, or where to find it. I don't even know if it really exists, or how—"

My aunt interrupted me with a little smile: "You should have asked your mother. She was a real expert in that area."

At that moment, my heart touched my ribs and pushed everything out of place. I picked up the slice of turkey, threw it to the floor, and ground it hard under my shoe. "I hate meat!" I shouted. "I hate it!" And I left the house, violently slamming the door.

It was cold, and I hadn't taken my jacket. My aunt's bike was leaning against the wall. I climbed onto it and started pedaling. I didn't know where to go, I only felt incredible strength in my legs.

In the sky were a few clouds and a few stars.

The little wheel of the generator made a whirring sound against the rim of the bicycle wheel. The beam from the headlight was weak, intermittent—it barely pierced the darkness of the night.

Almost without noticing, I reached the railroad station. It was a few minutes before ten, and the little bar was still open. I went in and said, "Give me a grappa."

It was the first time in my life that I'd ordered anything other than hot chocolate.

The first sip made me cough, and so did the second. With the third, I felt my legs growing slack. The lights of a flipper machine were shining in a corner.

"What time's the next train?" I asked.

"The last train has already left," the man behind the bar replied, washing some glasses as he did so. "And the next one doesn't come until tomorrow morning."

He had a wide face with a big, droopy mustache. Maybe he's my father, I thought. Maybe Mama came to the station, just like me, afraid and running away from something, maybe she sat quietly in a corner and he pretended to comfort her against the bathroom wall with his enormous body. And nine months later I came into the world.

I had finished my drink, and I felt strange.

"Do you have any children?" I asked him stupidly.

"Unfortunately, no," he replied. "But I can tell you, all the same, that it's not good for you to be here at this time of night. I'm going to close the place now, and you're going to go back home, OK?"

He walked with me to the door and pulled down the rolling shutter. He had a tiny, decrepit Fiat; it took him quite a while to get it started. At every attempt, the muffler shook as though it was about to come off. At last he drove away, leaving a series of large white clouds in his wake.

Go back home? What was waiting for me at home? And suppose I went back to the boarding school instead?

There probably wouldn't be anyone there—all the nuns had gone to visit their families. Ever since the scene with the firebrand, I hadn't dared to rebel against my aunt and uncle so openly again. At worst I had been a little rude. How would they receive me now? The truth was, I had always been an unwelcome guest.

I raised my eyes and saw a satellite crossing the sky like the star of Bethlehem. It was the night before Christmas. Maybe my fears were pointless. Maybe the star, with its fiery tail, had warmed even the hearts of my aunt and uncle. I'd ring the doorbell, and for the first time they'd welcome me with open arms.

I was already pedaling toward the house when I heard a voice calling me. It was the underwear salesman. He was sitting among his big bags of merchandise and smoking.

"It's you," I said.

He gave me a sign to sit down and offered me his cigarette. One, two, three puffs. At the third, something seized my stomach and turned it upside down. Where was I? Was I on a boat? I felt as though I was being tossed about on the high seas, and I had to vomit. Everything was spinning around me. Yes, I *was* on a boat, and the boat was sinking, it was whirling into a maelstrom that would carry me to the bottom of the sea. "First time you smoke?" the Negro asked. His hand alighted on my leg, high up, near the groin.

All of a sudden, the maelstrom stopped turning and I burst out laughing. The night was black, the road was black, the underwear salesman was black. What color was the soul? Maybe it was black, too; that was why it had always given me the slip. Instead of sinking, now I was swaying. I held my hands out in front of me, the way you do when you play blind man's bluff. Where were the boundaries of everything? I couldn't find them anymore.

A train passed behind us. Its noise drowned out his words. What kind of smell was that smell? The smell of a forest, of a jungle, the smell of an animal pursued and in pursuit. His body was very close, so close that it was crushing mine. Was he trying to warm me up? If so, then why was he pressing so hard? I didn't feel like laughing anymore, I felt like crying. I saw the whites of his eyes; his hands had disappeared into the night. How many hands did he have? I seemed to feel them everywhere. When a kind of insistent slug entered my mouth, I snapped my teeth shut to defend myself.

All at once, I found myself lying on the ground. He was shouting things I didn't understand and spitting. Then a kick landed on my back.

Right after that, I was on the bike, pedaling.

I pedaled and pedaled into the night with the headlight off, and everything seemed absolutely still. My legs were as heavy as legs in nightmares, when you have to run away but nothing responds to your commands anymore. At first I got all sweaty. Then the sweat turned to ice. A car passed me, going very fast and angrily sounding its horn. I almost lost my balance. When I got off the bicycle again and looked around, I didn't recognize anything. Not a street sign, not a traffic light, not a barn.

Where was I going? And who was I? I contemplated

the fingers that were gripping the brakes—they looked like a stranger's fingers. What was my name? It was like trying to catch a fish with your hands, the more I pursued it, the more it slipped away from me. There wasn't anyone around for me to ask, "Do you know who I am?"

Suddenly, an enormous cavity formed inside me, and I roamed about in that cavity with my eyes and my mouth wide open, like a fish in an aquarium. I was the fish and its owner, too. I existed, and I watched myself existing. And even though I existed and I was watching myself exist, I still wasn't certain that I existed.

Then, all at once and all together, the church bells started to ring. That's what woke me up. It's Christmas, I said, and I'm Rosa. The Rosa who left home with turkey sticking to her feet, the Rosa that nobody wants, the Rosa who's all thorns and no flowers, the Rosa who just got kicked by a Negro. I looked around; at last I figured out where I was. And so I started pedaling again in the direction of the village.

If I hadn't smoked that cigarette, would everything have turned out differently? Who can say? I had grappa in my stomach, the first grappa of my life. With the help of the smoke, the grappa turned into dynamite.

I was pedaling angrily, not calmly. The bicycle light was still out, even though the generator kept on turning. What it was charging was not the headlight but the darkness in my heart. At every revolution of the chain, the confused sorrow, the vague sense of humiliation I felt was changing into hatred. It was a pure hatred, transparent and indestructible like the crystalline carbon of diamonds. This hatred rose into my mouth and transformed itself into words: I sped along the provincial highway, shouting, "Go to hell, all of you! Drop dead, you assholes, you bastards, you shits!"

What had happened was that my heart had touched my ribs and got stuck there, like a balloon in the branches of a tree. The slightest movement would have been enough to make it burst. My ribs were like knives. I breathed, and they dug into my flesh. The more I breathed, the more piercing the pain became. Maybe an abscess had formed on one of my ventricles and now, finally, it was being lanced.

The square in front of the parish church was filled with cars. The warm light of the candles filtered through the big church windows. I flung my bicycle to the ground. Had I found someone standing outside the door, I would have punched him. Nobody was there, so I kicked the door wide open.

Everything happened very fast. The church was full of people. Although it was the middle of the sermon, everyone turned to look at me. I crossed the central aisle in giant steps.

"You all make me sick!" I yelled. "Do you know why? Because you're tombs, filthy, disgusting tombs, full of dead men's bones!"

The priest's mouth was still open, and one of his arms was suspended in air. A few kids started to laugh. I went over to the crèche, snatched the infant out of the manger, and raised it above my head like a trophy.

"Do you know what this is?" I shouted, whirling it around. "Do you really want to know what it is? It's a stupid little statue!"

Nobody breathed; everyone was looking at me in great consternation.

"You're worshiping a statue!" I said, and then I flung it into the middle of the aisle. "Nothing but a statue!"

The sound of the baby shattering into pieces woke them up. They all made the sign of the cross. I saw my aunt collapse in the front pew as my uncle bounded out of it, eager to get his hands on me.

Father Firmato grabbed the candelabra and rushed toward me. I managed to escape through the side aisle on the left. As I dashed past the colored catechism poster, I tore it off the wall. The words on the poster, in big letters, were "Love is . . ." I threw it onto the votive candles. In less than a second, the flames blazed up. I was already at the door.

Before I went out, I turned and shouted again with all the breath in my lungs: "Listen, Firmato, you pig! If you loved Mary Magdalene, you'd kiss her, not vomit in her face!"

Then I jumped on the bike and went back home.

Did I want to die? Probably so. The house was empty. Some embers were still glowing in the fireplace.

Suddenly I had no idea what to do next. I felt drained. It wasn't my heart that was pounding anymore, it was my head. I felt a fierce pain between my eyes. Everything was spinning. I let myself fall into one of the cellophane-covered armchairs. What would happen now? Would the carabinieri come and arrest me? Or maybe my aunt would kill me, as she'd said to their sergeant that day, "with her own hands."

I was too exhausted to feel any kind of fear whatsoever. Nothing was going right, and therefore everything was going right. Not far off, a dog was howling sadly. From the highway came the sound of automobiles returning home.

"Mama. . . ." I said before I drifted off to sleep. It was a brief sleep, in which I dreamed that she had her arms around me. She hugged me tight, smiling, without a word. Then, all at once my aunt was standing over me, screaming and holding the fireplace tongs in her hand. When the tongs started thumping me, I realized that I wasn't dreaming anymore. Since I no longer wanted to die, I slithered off the chair and tried to escape.

"Don't let her get away, grab her!" she shouted to my uncle. He came crashing down on me like a rugby player. We slid to the floor and lay stretched out in the middle of the hall.

My aunt kept shouting, "I'll kill you! I'll kill you, you bastard daughter of Satan!" and kept on beating me with the tongs. She beat me the way she beat the quilts, striking blindly, furiously. I tried to cover my head with my arms. When I saw the blood, I started shouting, too.

"Kill me! Go on and kill me! That way I can take you to hell with me, after all!"

She gave me a few more whacks, each one weaker

than the last, and then she dashed the tongs to the floor, covered her face with her hands, and burst into tears.

The neighbors' dog was still barking.

I stayed in bed for two days. I didn't want to eat; I didn't want to do anything. Even moving one of my legs seemed impossible. Sometimes I slept, sometimes I watched the mildew stain on the ceiling.

In the afternoon of the second day, I heard the sergeant's voice down in the kitchen. He hadn't come to take me away, as I'd hoped, but only to say that Father Firmato, out of respect to my aunt's piety and faith, had dropped all charges against me. "In fact," he added, "everyone in the village feels great sympathy for you."

My aunt thanked him in a thin little voice. "And to think, I took her into my home only because I wanted to do a good deed. Without a father, and the orphan of that mother! And we're old to boot. We hoped that we could save her, Sergeant. You understand. And now we have to carry this cross."

Before he left, the sergeant said, "Be brave!"

On the third day, when my aunt and uncle had gone to the shopping center, I took the bottle of dessert liqueur and hid in the woodshed.

FOUR

OW MANY LAYERS of skin do our bodies have? There are first-degree, second-degree, and third-degree burns. You can run into something and get a slight abrasion, or it can literally take your skin off. The difference between the two possibilities are the same as the difference between a mild inconvenience and a fight for survival. Our skin helps our bodies breathe and serves to protect the layers of more fragile tissue.

As for me, how many layers did I have left?

Sitting on a sawhorse, I drank the liqueur and looked at my arm. There was skin in some spots, but none in others. It seemed that the pain should have been limited, but instead its tentacles ran all over me. Maybe now my face was naked, too. It wasn't pink anymore but scarlet red. It must have looked like the face of one of those Borneo monkeys. Or the devil's.

Was there a hell or not? If the void was over our heads, was the void also under our feet? Or was there rather a great imbalance between the two poles? Above, the sky, as light and crinkly as a tulle veil, and below, all the refuse, all the iron filings of the world? Maybe that was why the earth held together, because of the extraordinary weight at its center.

There was fire down there, and lead and tin and coal. And all the filthiest souls were there, too. They wallowed in the flames like pigs wallowing in mud. Without the weight at its center, our planet would be as light as a meringue. Very voluminous, but very light. Unable to maintain its course, even for a fraction of a second, it would veer off and explode like a snowball against an automobile window. Therefore, since we were still here, it necessarily followed that the center was heavy. Heavy and inhabited, as an apple is inhabited by a worm.

Every house has an owner. What sort of face did the proprietor of hell have? Was it the same one that dominated all our days?

When I tore down the catechism poster with "Love is . . ." written on it and dropped it on the candles, it caught fire immediately. It could have put up a modicum of resistance, struggled for a minute or so, before it let itself be consumed. That would have enabled people to say, "You see? Love can withstand fire. Or, at the very least, it tries to. . . ."

Love conquers all—there's a statement I'd heard many times. Love is stronger than death. But it wasn't true, because love, even if it exists, is flimsy. It's so flimsy it's practically invisible. And being invisible is almost the same as being nonexistent. If there's a big fire, you can see its smoke from miles away, and the burned site bears the marks of the flames for years. Love, on the other hand, remains invisible, even if it's under your nose.

I was burning, too. My body was burning, and I was burning inside. That was why I drank, to have some semblance of relief. But the relief was short-lived. I should have rolled around in the freezing snow, I should have screamed out, in my most dreadful voice, the things that were in my heart.

Hate was my favorite word. I took to repeating it, over and over, under my breath. I hate you singular. I hate you plural. I hate myself. I hate you singular. I hate you plural. I hate myself. Then I took away the pronouns, and all that remained was *hate*.

Òdio. Separating the letters, I changed it to *O dìo.* Oh God.

Why was everyone afraid of going to hell? I was much more scared by the thought of going to heaven. I could put up with Satan's countenance, but God's! Absolutely impossible. He'd see my littleness. He'd despise me the way my aunt and the priest despised me. I had, after all, broken the statue of Baby Jesus. I'd broken it on the most sacred of nights, the night when he was born. Even if another world existed, where would I ever be able to go?

That night, in bed, I thought: just as there are prayers that you can say to angels, there are some that you

39

can say to the devil, too. I tried to recite the Angelus, changing the invocation. But I wasn't able to fall asleep. I imagined that the stain on the ceiling had a thousand eyes, fluorescent eyes, and tongues like shining arrows shot into the darkness of the room. I was awakened in the middle of the night by the sound of my voice. I was screaming. For a minute it seemed that the stain on the ceiling was a big monkey, with a blood-smeared mouth and eyes like burning coals, about to jump on me.

I passed the rest of the holidays closed up in my room, like a stowaway on a ship. As soon as they left the house, I went down to the kitchen.

On the fourth of January, I decided to go back to my boarding school. My aunt was in the henhouse when I announced my decision to her. She said neither "Yes" nor "No" nor "Have a good trip." She didn't even raise her eyes from the bucket of chicken feed.

I stuffed my few things in a bag. The bus was leaving at noon. My uncle was out hunting. When my aunt left to go to the market, I put rat poison in the food for the rabbits and the chickens.

"Are you here already?" said the mother superior when she saw me arrive.

We went into her office. An electric kettle was boiling in a corner. The nun turned it off, poured the water into a teapot, and sat down across from me.

"Has something happened?" she asked me.

I shrugged my shoulders. "Absolutely nothing. I was bored."

She was staring at me insistently, and I began to feel uneasy.

"What's wrong with your head?"

"I fell off my bicycle."

The pendulum clock behind her desk struck a quarter past four. It was almost dark outside. The mother superior's hand lightly touched mine. Her voice was low and calm.

"Rosa, why don't you tell the truth? You have nothing to fear from me."

"Truth doesn't exist."

"Are you sure about that?"

In answer, I said the first thing that came to my mind. "Nobody loves me. It makes no difference whether I live or die."

"You're mistaken. I love you."

"All you care about is collecting your fees."

"What can I do to make you change your mind?"

"Nothing."

"Shall I call the psychologist?"

"I detest psychologists."

"Well, what then?"

"Everything's all right the way it is."

"I don't believe everything's all right."

"But I say it is, and that's the end of it."

At that point, I felt her hands on mine. They were small and rather cold.

"Why don't you look me in the eyes?"

"That's not mandatory."

"It's not mandatory, but it would be nice."

"I couldn't care less about being nice."

At that instant, the rosary bell rang. The mother superior got to her feet.

"I must go, but before you leave there are two things I want to tell you. This is the first: the door to my office and the door to my room are always open, both day and night. If you have an urge to talk, just open the door and come in. . . ."

"What's the second thing?"

"Remember that you have no responsibility for your past, but you have a great deal where your future is concerned. Your future is in your hands, and it's up to you to build it. That's why I'm inviting you to think things over and open your heart before you do something foolish."

The following months were months of darkness, ripped apart from time to time by sudden, exceedingly violent flashes of light. Everything seemed useless, and I couldn't bear anyone's company. I attended classes without hearing a single word the teachers said. I spent hours poring over books, but they were nothing but a stream of opaque pages, one after another, flowing past my eyes. I was only a year from graduation, but that fact failed to give me any joy.

My future was like the pages: opaque.

I'd probably go back to the farm and pass the rest of my days cleaning up rabbit and chicken shit. Eventually, my aunt and uncle would die and everything would pass into my hands, but it would be too late. By then I'd be old and ugly, I'd never find anyone to live with me. Maybe one day I'd give up everything and take up residence on the street with the stray dogs. At least they would love me. Or maybe I wouldn't do any of that. I'd simply remain on the farm, and year after year the fog would enter me and consume my bones. Alcohol would take care of consuming my brain. There would be nothing between my ears but a darkness as deep as inside the hold of a ship. Only one idea would circulate in there, an idea as old as the world: the best way to be done with it. And so one day, dragging my feet, I'd go out to the woodshed and hang myself from the highest beam. The newspapers would dedicate a scant paragraph to my demise: DERANGED WOMAN FOUND DEAD IN HER HOME.

Meanwhile I was surrounded by my schoolmates, who talked only about their own futures. Some planned to get married, others dreamed of attending a university. One wanted to be a nurse, another to join the forest service. It was said that the shiest and most silent girl among us wished to take vows and remain closed up in that place forever. I didn't tell anyone what I was thinking. If anyone questioned me, I gave the most banal answers: I'll study computer science, I'll help my aunt and uncle in the country.

At times it happens that a previously nonexistent island rises out of the sea, or that lava from a volcano creates or obliterates an entire region. Something similar was happening to me, except that what was being born inside me was not an island, but a swamp. It was a swamp without dawns or sunsets; no wind rustled its reeds or stirred the leafy branches of its willow trees. The air around it was dark and still. Its oozy mud was in ferment, emitting miasmas into the dark, still air. During the night I felt these emanations slowly issuing from the orifices of my body. There was an odor of methane, an odor of sulfur, an odor of something rotting deep inside me.

Winter passed, and the days started to grow longer. The sparrows and the blackbirds darted busily from one part of the garden to another, while the buds were already beginning to swell on their branches. The first flowers— the purple violets, the bright yellow primroses—appeared amid the grass in the ditches and on the slopes. Everything even lightly touched by the sun was returning to life. With the change of seasons, the fermentation of the swamp had produced some forms of energy as well. Hadn't the same thing happened, perhaps, at the dawn of the world? At certain moments, in pools without oxygen, the amino acids curdled and gave rise to life. They didn't curdle by themselves, but with the aid of lightning. A bolt of lightning struck the water and caused the short circuit. Lightning was also beginning to strike inside me, the bolts whistled and exploded like fireworks on New Year's Eve. For an instant their white light rent the veil of darkness. I walked down the long halls and wondered, how much longer will I be able to keep this terrible energy hidden?

The short circuit arrived during mass on Easter Sunday. All at once, in the middle of the Offertory, the lightning bolts abandoned their ususal trajectory. Instead of plunging into the swamp, where they would be quenched, they took aim at my head. In a fraction of a second I saw everything and went blind, heard everything and went deaf. Inside me there was power, energy, devastation. I ran to the wall and beat my head against it. Which would win the day, my forehead or the masonry? In that moment I was looking for a switch to throw, a button to press, something that might damp the current. I was looking for it and not looking for it.

When a hand tried to stop me, the first thing I did was to bite it. The ceremony was interrupted. Someone shouted, "Quick, get a doctor!" I heard someone running toward the exit, screaming. Then something entered my body—a needle, most likely. What had been fire rapidly turned into fog. I am hate, I am fury, I thought before I was swallowed up. I am myself and not myself. Pure destructive will.

FIVE

I was in the hospital for four days. My electroencephalogram results were absolutely perfect. Every morning a doctor came and asked me, "Are you sure you didn't take some drug? And maybe a few drinks on top of that?" But they tested me, and I was clean.

The nuns also asked me questions. They wondered: had I suffered a head injury in the past? "Sure," I said. "During the Christmas holidays. I fell off my bicycle." I'd never had much talent for telling lies, but all of a sudden I had become quite good at it. I knew how to dupe other people, how to manipulate them. I knew how to put on an innocent face while terrible thoughts were flashing through my mind. For the first time in my life, I felt secure, capable, powerful. When I was alone, I repeated a precept to myself: lying and holding the world in the palm of your hand are two sides of the same coin.

After I returned to the boarding school, I became the calmest, the most devout of the students. When it was time for the rosary, I ran to the chapel before anyone else; during evening prayers, my voice dominated all the others in the dormitory. In church, when we genuflected before the tabernacle, I was the only one whose knee touched the floor.

I could do this, I could allow myself to do this, because now I knew that it was an empty gesture. The crucifix was a statue, and the receptacle under it held nothing but a few wafers of bread. Bowing before that and bowing before a box of laundry detergent were exactly the same thing.

I felt that now there was harmony between my thought and the look in my eyes. One was a steel blade, the other was its cutting edge. Love didn't matter to me at all anymore; it was a totem adored by too many people, and like all totems it was hollow. What did matter was that I should be strong, that I should be able to take control of my life and to direct it in such a way as to extract from it the maximum benefit.

Lucidity—seeing things as they are and not as one would wish them to be—was my strong point. During mass, when I looked around and saw all those bowed heads, I had to make a mighty effort not to burst out laughing. All in all, I thought as I pressed my lips together, this must be compassion: to understand that these girls are just poor wretches, the only life they know is a slave's life, and therefore they need to believe that there's someone in heaven. When the moment came for the Our Father, I raised my open hands as though I were expecting manna to fall and said, "Our Father, who art not in heaven nor anywhere else . . ."

Naturally, I wanted something more. I wanted absolute certainty that the whole thing was a con game. I had already traveled down many hard roads, but up to this point I had failed to take the hardest of them all: cold-blooded sacrilege. At midnight mass on Christmas Eve, at the moment when I flung down the infant Jesus, I had been smoking dope and drinking alcohol; there wasn't any science in my gesture, only anger. Now I intended to make a flawless demonstration of my theory.

God can kill whomever he wishes, and in a thousand different ways; the whole Bible offers proof of that in black and white. If God exists, I told myself, he'll afflict me with some dreadful punishment. If, on the other hand, he doesn't exist, nothing at all will happen to me.

I went to the mother superior's office in the middle of the night. She'd told me the truth—her door was always open. Not finding anything of interest on her table, I searched through her drawers. There I had better luck; I found a shabby, much used rosary and a little wooden cross with "Jerusalem" written on it.

I took these items directly to the toilet and flushed them down.

Back in my bed, I fell into a deep, dreamless sleep.

A week later, the toilet backed up. The plumber came and took it apart. He fished out the rosary and the cross, wrapped up in toilet paper as though in a bridal veil.

A mantle of ice spread over the boarding school.

There were interrogation sessions, meetings with the father confessor, intensive investigations. I myself was amazed by my ability to lie, by the naturalness with which I did it.

For ten days, no one talked about anything else. There was a ceremony to reconsecrate the desecrated objects. Then this matter, too, sank into oblivion.

I went back to the mother superior's office early in June. This time, she summoned me. I was convinced that it would be a routine visit, the usual chat before summer vacation. Instead, immediately after asking me to sit down, she said, "I'm sorry to tell you this, Rosa, but we can't keep you here anymore."

This was followed by a long silence. The scent of jasmine wafted in through the open window.

I should have asked, "Why?" but I didn't feel like it. When I opened my mouth, all I said was "All right."

"Until you come of age, you'll stay with your aunt and uncle. . . ."

"All right."

The mother superior sat facing me. I could tell from her eyes that she'd grown old. Once again I felt her small, cold hands on mine.

"Don't you want to say anything else?"

"What should I say? You others have made this decision, not me."

"Why don't you open your heart to me?"

"Hearts are boxes?"

"Boxes with something inside."

"Mine's empty."

"Permit me not to believe you."

"You're free to believe or not believe whatever you want."

"Rosa, aren't you hiding something from me? I'm very worried about you."

"Seeing that I'm about to go away, my life doesn't concern you anymore."

"The first time I took your hand you were almost eight."

I was starting to get tired of this.

"Be patient," I said, rising to my feet. "All things pass."

"Love doesn't pass," she replied, following me to the door. She clasped me with her thin hands. "Remember that I'm always here, waiting for you. No matter what you tell me, I'll accept it."

She was pathetic.

"All right," I answered stiffly.

"At least give me a hug, let me kiss you."

I bent down to her height. The skin of her cheeks was soft and cool.

My aunt and uncle received me in silence. I matched their silence with my own. There were no more demands that I go to church, I was no longer required to display good manners, everybody expected the worst from me. I didn't have any difficulty giving it to them.

Instead of running downstairs to help my aunt every morning, I slept late. By the time I went down for breakfast, they were having lunch. Turkey Neck's nostrils flared with rage, but instead of taking me by the throat, she kept quiet. I'd said to her, the day I got back, "If you ever so much as lay a finger on me, I'll cause such a scandal that you'll have to move to another town for shame." That was why she stayed where she was, unmoving, with her mouth closed, and as soon as I went out she picked a fight with her husband. I was *his* niece, after all, he'd been the one to bring this cross into their home. The little orphan girl she'd adopted out of Christian charity, and who should have been eternally grateful to her, had turned on her like a snake with its fangs full of poison.

When the sun started to lose a little of its force, I'd take my aunt's bicycle and go riding along the white roads. I'd ride around until dusk so I could see the fireflies, and often I'd stay out to look at the stars, too.

Whenever I got back home, my aunt and uncle would have already been asleep for some time. Even if my uncle wanted to stay up, my aunt dragged him to bed early every night. I went into the parlor and opened the little liquor cabinet. There were three or four bottles, they'd been there for years, gifts from people who were probably dead by now. I started with the Vecchia Romagna and moved on to the Amaretto. Stretching out on the sofa, I felt warm at last. It wasn't the external warmth of the August sun but a warmth that came from within, the same warmth that used to be in the shower of kisses.

After two weeks, the bottles were empty. I'd come home, and I'd need a drink. So I started taking money out of my uncle's jacket. When he noticed and hid his wallet, I began making the rounds of the churches in the neighboring villages. I carried with me a piece of twisted wire, which I threaded through the slots in the poor boxes. After one or two afternoons of such work, I could always manage to buy another bottle of liquor.

In September I should have signed up for some classes and made an effort to finish high school, one way or another. In reality, however, I had but one thought in my mind: I wanted to come of age. I felt like a sprinter waiting for the starter's pistol to fire, with my muscles tensed and my eyes fixed on the finish line. I wanted to go far, to show them all what I was capable of.

I would reach my majority at the end of December. Halfway through October, I began to organize my escape.

After a month, responding to an ad in the newspaper, I found a way out. A family in the nearby city was looking for someone to work as an au pair. I would have to take care of a little girl, accompany her to school and the swimming pool. In exchange I would have a room all my own with a private bath, as well as a small salary and the option of taking a course to continue my education. I went to meet the family, and we liked one another. I was to start work in January, after they returned from their skiing holiday. Of course, I hadn't said anything to my aunt and uncle. I'd waited quietly for months, as patient as a spider spinning its web.

The day before my departure, I bought a bottle of sparkling wine. I put it on the table, together with two glasses and a note, just before I left the house. The note read: "You can drink a toast at last. The cross is going away on her own two legs."

Outside it was still dark. The commuters' automobiles were already hurrying down the highway.

A church bell rang somewhere. The neighbors' dog kept barking until I was out of sight.

SIX

FEW THINGS in the world are as delicate as house-plants. A slight change in exposure, an infinitesimal draft can be enough to shift them from flourishing luxuriance to death in the course of a few days.

My new home, a double penthouse apartment with many windows set into the roof, was filled with plants. A small forest was growing under every sliver of light.

Giulia, my little charge's mother, loved those plants, and shortly after I arrived the first thing she did was to teach me how to take care of them. As I watered them and polished their leaves, I couldn't help thinking about the sad, yellowish, stunted plants that grew in the boarding school. A dusty philodendron, drooping down from the top of an armoire. A wandering Jew, languishing in a pot at the end of a corridor.

Plants reflect the place where they live, but they also reveal something about the people they live with. In the boarding school, nobody cared a thing about them; here, on the other hand, they were treated with love.

As the days passed, I realized that what happens to

plants isn't much different from what happens to people. When I was with the nuns, I was one of their plants, a drab plant with pale leaves. At my aunt and uncle's, I was a plant that was dying of thirst; they had acquired me in the belief that I was made of plastic. In my new home, however, I was a plant that soaked up light. The light penetrated me and evaporated the fog, the air entered my pores and drove out the dust. In the morning, I'd look at myself in the mirror and repeat my name. "Rosa," I'd say softly, as if I were seeing myself for the first time.

For years I had been like a cooking pot with its lid on. I boiled and boiled, and the condensation remained inside. Now the condensation was slowly disappearing. I was hearing new kinds of discourse, I was discovering a different approach to life. I listened, and I knew that this was the right way to live, the way that should have been mine from the beginning.

During my first days in her house, Signora Giulia followed my every move. She wanted to see how I handled myself in the kitchen. She taught me how to prepare her daughter's three or four favorite dishes. She assessed my ability to help the child with her homework. Since everything went well, after a week she left me on my own and went back to her teaching job.

We liked each other instantly. She was very affectionate toward me, and I responded to her affection by trying to carry out my duties in the best possible way. I don't know how old she might have been, certainly over forty, because she had quite a few gray hairs. Once, while stirring a risotto, she said, "I thought about having children only at the last minute." Her husband must have been her age, more or less, maybe a few years older. Signora Giulia told me they had met when they were attending the university. Now he was a famous architect, and he had a large studio where he often worked late into the night. He was tall and elegant, with a very well-groomed beard. Along with architecture, music was his great passion. When he was home, the sound of his powerful stereo invaded every room.

I ate lunch and dinner with them, and in the evening we all sat on the same sofa and watched television. After a few weeks, I even started participating in their conversations. They'd ask me, "What do you think about that, Rosa?" and I'd answer freely. Neither of them laughed when I spoke; in fact, they seemed to listen to me with a certain interest. For the first time, I felt that my ideas were worthy of respect and didn't seem totally out of place alongside those of normal persons.

Annalisa was the little girl's name, and I had a mansard room next to hers. There was a dormer window right above my bed, so at night, if I wasn't able to fall asleep, I could look at the sky.

By now, the farm and the boarding school existed in a different galaxy; I saw them as small, far off, harmless. They had disappeared from my life, and they were about to disappear from my memory. Now I was part of the right family, the one I should have been born into.

I watched the sky, and then, under the covers, I repeated the words that had been forbidden to me since what felt like forever. Daddy. Mama. Daddy.

What had happened to the girl who used to get drunk in the living room every night? The girl who, for more than ten years, had lived as a prisoner between the bleakness of the farm and the gloom of the boarding school? I could just barely glimpse a few traces of the hatred that had dominated my heart for so long. It was like a thunderstorm that vents its rage for a while, evoking the end of the world, and then suddenly stops and hurries off to some other location. It leaves behind wet grass, a couple of smoldering trees, but the storm itself is already far away. That thin violet line fleeing toward the horizon isn't scary anymore.

The only thing in that house that bothered me a bit was the child. They had spoiled her terribly. All she had to do was lift a finger and point at something, and right away it was hers. Her mother was constantly hugging her as though she wanted to crush her. "I know I'm making a mistake," Signora Giulia said. "But I can't help myself. When you become a parent so late in life, you're something of a grandparent, too."

Annalisa was arrogant and nervous. When we were alone, she treated me like an old shoe. Naturally, I wouldn't stand for that, and if no one was looking I squeezed her wrists hard. Not to hurt her, just to let her know who was in charge of our game.

One morning we went downtown to a big department store to upgrade her wardrobe. Passing in front of a mirror, I felt a little ashamed. She looked like the princess; I looked like Cinderella. I was still wearing the clothes from the farm and boarding school. In the pitiless light inside the store, they revealed their true nature. They were rags.

The saleslady was obliged to show us dozens of outfits. As Annalisa's mother tried them on her, the child steadily became more and more tired, and more and more contrary.

"How does it look to you, Rosa?" Signora Giulia asked me from time to time, and I gave my opinion in reply. Too big. Too showy. Not right for her.

After a pile of about ten items had accumulated on the counter, the saleslady asked, "Will there be anything else?"

"No, that's enough," Signora Giulia said.

"Shall we move on to the young lady?"

My cheeks suddenly started burning as though I had run a great distance. She had mistaken me for Annalisa's sister. How would Signora Giulia answer her? "Oh no, this has nothing to do with her, she works for me"? Or maybe . . .

I was keeping my eyes down when I heard her say, "But of course. Let's move on to the young lady."

We had to go to a different department. As we walked across the store, I felt as though I were drunk. I was unsteady, awkward.

The saleslady drew back the sliding door of a large closet. While she was picking out some dresses, she began chatting with Signora Giulia.

"Young people are all like that these days. All they

want is secondhand stuff. The better off their families are, the more they like to look like ragamuffins. You may not believe me, madam, but I've seen mothers begging their daughters to accept a dress. That's how we are, we copy everything from the Americans. All the worst things, I mean."

Then she took out a lovely cotton dress, cornflower blue, and held it up against me. "What do you think about this one? Shall we try something a little bit brighter?"

"Yes, let's have more color," Signora Giulia said, nodding. "Something in green. A green that goes with her eyes."

I tried on four or five dresses. Every time I came out of the dressing room, I felt like a different person. At one point, Signora Giulia stepped to my side and pulled back my hair, looking at me in the mirror. "You see how pretty you are when you give yourself a chance!"

We left the store carrying two bags, one for me and one for Annalisa.

For the first time in my life, I started noticing the way I looked. Up until then, I'd paid attention to my inside only, not my outside. I'd never thought that there could be anything important about how other people saw me. Now I began to realize that I was neither too thin nor too fat. I wasn't extremely tall, but I wasn't short, either. If I let my hair fall loose on my shoulders and looked at myself in the mirror, I saw before me a beautiful girl.

Shortly after the visit to the store, Signora Giulia started to insist that I take up my schooling again. She continually repeated, "You've got only a year left, it's a shame to throw it all away. Besides, with your brains, you can't want to be a nanny all your life!"

I thought about it for a while and decided she was right. I was at a point where many doors were opening for me; what sense did it make to let them close? I wasn't surrounded by walls anymore. I could go to college, I could study literature or philosophy or medicine. Everyone had expected me to turn out bad—to turn out, that is, like my mother—and instead I would become somebody important. A great doctor. A philosopher interviewed in all the newspapers.

The following week, I started attending evening school. All the other people in class were adults, and I found that I felt perfectly at ease. I took the bus to school, and the architect often picked me up when the classes were over. His studio was in the same part of the city, and it wasn't unusual for him to stay there late into the evening.

The first few times, I was very intimidated. I got into the car in silence, and I remained silent all the way home. I didn't have the same confidence with him as I had with his wife. I'd never had men in my life, except for my uncle, and he was more of a husk than a man. In any case, as I sat beside the architect I felt that something strange was happening. If he asked me a question, my voice came out sounding too high or too low. If he looked at me, I sweated like a fountain.

Did he notice how shy I was? I don't know. He drove with calm, deliberate movements; his entire concentration seemed to be fixed on the road. He'd brake, the car would idle, he'd shift gears, we'd drive on.

Then, one evening when we were stopped at a traffic light, he turned to me and said, "Say, why don't you tell me a little about yourself?"

I wasn't ready for such a question, so I mumbled a few halting phrases. I needed time to construct a lie. Then the barrier fell, and my words flowed out naturally. My father had died in an accident shortly before I was born. He was a policeman, and a truck had gone out of control and run him down at a checkpoint on the highway. My mother was a Latin teacher. One day, as she was returning home from school, she'd had a seizure and gone off the road. Thus, at a little more than seven years old, I was a complete orphan. I had an aunt and an uncle—good, hardworking people—but they were very old and couldn't keep me with them. And so I had grown up in a boarding school.

From time to time, as I told my story, he made brief comments: "Really?" "Go on!" "What awful luck!" After I came to the end, he asked me, "And how did you like your boarding school?"

"It was a very beautiful place," I replied. "I had my own room, with a private bath and a view overlooking an extremely elegant park. There were tennis courts and an indoor swimming pool. The only trouble was . . ."

"Was what?"

"I never could believe those stories they told us."

"What stories?"

"The nuns' stories. Jesus and all the rest. Heaven and hell. Those tales that were invented to make us behave. In the beginning, when I was little, I sort of believed them. But as soon as I grew up, I saw that the whole thing was a con game."

The architect turned and looked at me.

"A 'con game,' " he repeated, laughing. "Listen to this kid!"

The following week, while I was waiting for the bus to take me to school, he passed by the stop. He opened the car door and said, "Aren't you getting in?"

I thought he was going to give me a ride to school, but as soon as I pulled the door closed he said gaily, "Today you're playing hooky! Let's go for a drive!"

I tried to protest: it wasn't long before the exams, I didn't like to miss class.

He shut me up right away. "You're such a good student. How can it matter if you skip class this one time?"

He took me to a restaurant in the hills outside the city. It was the end of April, and the air was still too damp to dine outdoors, so we sat at a table on a kind of enclosed porch. We had a red-and-white-checked tablecloth; few of the tables around us were occupied. He ordered wine. I drank a glass, and since my stomach was empty the wine immediately went to my head.

He sipped slowly from his own glass, staring directly

into my eyes. Then, in a voice pitched lower than usual, he said, "Do you know that I find you fascinating? You're so young, and you have so many ideas. The other evening you told me a few things about yourself. Tell me some more."

"Like what?"

"I don't know. Talk about the con game, for example."

I drank another glass and started talking again. I began at the beginning, at Jesus with his heart in his hand who hadn't protected me and had protected my mother even less. Then I continued with the crucifix in the boarding school that listened to everybody's prayers and never answered any. By the time they brought the tagliatelle, I had moved on to Father Firmato and the Christmas midnight mass.

The architect was so absorbed in what I was saying that he practically forgot to eat; if I stopped for a moment, he'd urge me on at once: "And then?" Eventually I came to my modified versions of the Angelus and the Lord's Prayer, which I'd murmured every night in the silence of my room. Next I told him, in elaborate detail, the story of the rosary in the toilet. The fact that I was still alive provided the perfect demonstration of my theory. Heaven was empty space.

Apparently enraptured by my words, at times he shook his head, at others he burst out laughing. "I can't believe it! Did you really do that?" Thus encouraged, I expatiated on my subject, pleased to add even more details.

Before they brought our desserts, he gently brushed my hand with his fingertips. "You know, you're a truly extraordinary person. You're so young, and already your thinking is so liberated. I was nearly thirty before I reached your level of clarity. It took until then for me to realize that the only life worth living is one in which you set no boundaries for yourself. You have to open the door and toss out all your qualms and all your feelings of guilt. Isn't that right?"

"Of course!" I replied, in the voice of a professor bringing her class to an end.

That night, as I lay in bed, I felt once again the sensation of warmth rising up inside me. I had spent so many years without a father. Now I was glad that I'd had to wait so long. I wouldn't have been able to find a better one. The architect—whom I called Franco from that time on— approved of everything I said, just as I was in agreement with every word that issued from his mouth. We really did seem like father and daughter.

Before I fell asleep, I reflected that adoption didn't seem like such a crazy idea anymore. Probably, at some time not very far in the future, my aunt and uncle would go off to hell and I'd be free to become someone else's daughter. It was true that Giulia and Franco had one already, but she'd never give them the satisfaction that I could give. In fact, she seemed pretty stupid. And besides, she was too capricious to succeed in putting together two consecutive thoughts.

Did Signora Giulia know that the two of us went out for dinner alone every now and then? When we got back home after the second time, I would have liked to ask her that question, but then—I don't know why—it died in my throat. Even when I was alone with her, I never could say, "You know, last night I went to dinner with your husband." I had a deep, intense relationship with each of them, although in different ways. For this reason, I felt that it was right to keep them distinct.

Early in May, Franco left to teach a two-week course at a foreign university. During that time, Signora Giulia was hardly ever home. She'd call around seven in the evening and say in an amused voice, "Rosa, I'm staying out tonight, too. Give Annalisa some pasta, as usual."

I felt plagued by an uneasiness that was completely new. I still didn't know that love is not a satin ribbon that adorns your wrists, but a chain that saws at them.

I'd put Annalisa to bed as early as possible and then go into Franco's studio to sniff his things, his pens, his pencils, his sheets of paper. With the help of the smells, I was able to reconstruct his face and the warmth of his voice. I sat in his chair, picked up his books, and opened them. They weren't architecture books, they were books of philosophy. In some of them, many passages were underlined. I read them and realized that they were the very same passages that I would have underlined myself.

On the night of his return, Franco came to pick me up at school. He pulled into a side street, stopped the car, and handed me two packages.

"For you," he said.

They were the first gifts I'd received since my aunt and uncle's white blouses. I felt confused.

"Shall I open them now?"

"Of course."

I unwrapped the bigger one first. There was a sweat-shirt inside. It was black, with a colored drawing of the Eiffel Tower on the front and "Paris" written underneath.

"Oh, thank you," I said, kissing him on the cheeks. "It's beautiful."

Then I started to unwrap the second package. "What can it be?"

He was smiling. "Open it and you'll see."

The wrapping paper was Bordeaux red and as light as tissue paper. My fingers slid over it with great ease. I glimpsed two soft, white objects and lifted them up. I was holding a brassiere and a garter belt, both in white lace.

"Do you like them?" he asked, bringing his face close to mine. "I saw them in a shop window, and I thought you'd probably never had anything of the sort. I'm not a girl, but I believe there's a certain pleasure in knowing you look beautiful under your clothes, too. Am I right?"

"I think so."

"You don't seem very enthusiastic."

"But I am."

"In any case, if you don't like them, you're under no

obligation to wear them. You can leave them in your drawer or give them away."

He put the car in gear and started driving in silence, his eyes fixed on the road in front of him.

Maybe I'd inadvertently offended him. I picked up the lingerie again.

"They're really beautiful! I can't wait to put them on. What are they, silk?"

"Yes, silk."

The warm, scented air of May was coming in through the open window. I wanted to take my time and make up for the offense I'd given him.

"Let's go get some ice cream," I suggested.

A short while later, we were seated outside an ice-cream parlor in a residential neighborhood. I no longer had the urge for something cool and sweet, so I ordered a whiskey.

"Are you sure you know what you're doing?" he asked. And then, at last, he smiled again.

It was months since I'd drunk hard liquor. I hadn't had any dinner, and my stomach began to burn after the first few sips. The glass seemed small to me, and so, as soon as it was empty, I ordered another one.

Franco took my hand in his. He had tapering fingers, strong, soft, and warm. Leaning close to my ear, he whispered, "Are you trying to forget something?"

A jasmine plant was growing in a pot behind us. Its flowers had opened, and their odor was so strong it made me nauseous. In front of us, a group of boys were straddling their motorbikes. While some of them smoked cigarettes, others licked their ice-cream cones.

Before I spoke, I let my eyes slide sideways and fix on a dark patch in the night. Then I opened my mouth and began: "My mother wasn't a Latin teacher, she was a whore. She got run over while she was standing next to a signal fire on a highway. . . ."

That night I should have felt inside me the sensation of lightness that follows the accomplishment of great exploits. After all, for the first time in my life I had freed myself from a burden. From *the* burden, in fact. I should have plunged at once into a happy, undisturbed sleep. But instead, as soon as I turned out the light, anxiety started to consume me. Why had I spoken? To feel more protected? And why did I think I needed to be more protected? What was threatening me?

Although I didn't have the courage to admit it, in some part of me, deep down, I was already beginning to regret what I'd done. How could I have even considered telling my secret? That secret was the engine of my strength, the furious will that allowed me to overcome every obstacle and avoid attachment to anything. Now my secret was public, it was in the possession of another person, who could go around telling it to everyone. Maybe Franco himself has already started to despise me, I thought. If we should meet in the kitchen tomorrow morning, he won't even raise his eyes to tell me hello.

Swollen, whitish clouds had appeared in the frame of the dormer window. They were moving fast, and within a few minutes they covered the moon and the stars. It'll rain tomorrow, I thought, and all at once I understood. Love is putting yourself at someone else's mercy, with no possibility of self-defense.

SEVEN

I WAS SCHEDULED to take the final examination for my high school diploma in a little more than a month. At the dinner table, we discussed what I would do afterward. Signora Giulia and Franco were not opposed to my continuing my education. Annalisa went to school in the morning, and therefore I was completely free.

Because I knew nothing about mathematics, I saw that I must, with great reluctance, forget about majoring in architecture. My choice was between languages and philosophy.

Signora Giulia insisted that I should study modern languages. If you know several languages, she said, you can work in many different fields, and besides you can move around, travel to different places.

Franco, on the other hand, favored philosophy. "It would be a real sin to waste that mind of yours. . . ." According to him, I would find the most self-fulfillment in philosophy courses, because I liked speculating about the big questions and I was capable of doing so with an open-mindedness that was very rare in a person so young.

Franco loved that side of my character. In order to be loved even more, I learned to emphasize it. I asked to borrow some of his philosophy books. Instead of studying, I spent my time reading them, and at night we'd stay up late discussing them.

One day he said to me, "You've had the great privilege of growing up without love. Because of that, you got your freedom at an early age. You look at things and see them as they are. You feel no need to construct bizarre theories about them."

"Love is a toxic substance," he often said. "It poisons you by compelling you, always, willy-nilly, to do what you don't want to do. Whereas people like you are free. You're there, and you go forward. You overcome everything, like an icebreaker."

One day I answered him back. "But you got married," I said.

He burst out laughing. "Love and marriage are not the same thing! People get married for money, for company, for biology, but surely not for love. Why do you think Giulia and I get along so well? Because from the very beginning we made sure we were clear on this point. We were fond of one another, and both of us wanted a child. For the rest, we're completely free."

I listened to him and nodded, nodded and listened. I never tired of talking with him. I felt superior, far from everything and everybody else, protected by the affection of the older man, practically a father, who was by my side.

Around the middle of June, Annalisa and Signora Giulia went to the beach for a week. School was out.

The day they left, Franco invited me to dinner at a friend's house. The friend was a philosophy professor, and Franco thought that talking with this man would help me clarify my ideas about my future. I found this very considerate of him.

I had the afternoon off, so I took my time getting myself ready. After a long, cool shower, I carefully selected my clothes for the evening. I hadn't yet worn the Parisian lingerie, and this seemed like the best occasion for it.

Before we left the house, Franco proposed an aperitif on the terrace. The air was warm, loaded with the scents that herald the coming of summer. Over our heads, hurtling like crisscrossing arrows, were dozens and dozens of house martins.

"As you'll see," he told me, "Aldo's an incredible fellow. You'll like him. We've known each other since we were boys."

A half hour later, we arrived at the friend's apartment. He had a penthouse, too, but no terrace.

The first thing that struck me about him was how ugly he was—short, fat, and bald, with a face still marked by the acne of his younger days. He looked like one of those toads that doze under rocks in the winter. But he was very nice. He gave me a warm handshake, saying, "So this is the famous Rosa!" and then went on talking at machine-gun speed. "Which wine should we start with? The red or the white? Perhaps you'd prefer an Aperol or a Campari? Shall we sit down to eat right away, or would you like to relax for a bit in the living room?"

"This is Rosa's evening," Franco said. "It's up to her to decide."

I tried a weak protest: "It's not even close to my birthday."

Aldo burst out laughing. He laughed the same way he spoke.

"But it is, in a way. When you leave the world of adolescence and become an adult, isn't that a kind of birthday?"

"In a few months you'll be a first-year philosophy student at the university," Franco elaborated, "and therefore everything will change."

"In that case, white wine," I said.

They toasted me at once. "To your studies!" they said, raising their glasses. "To your life!"

Shortly after that, we took our seats at the dining table.

Aldo wasn't married. The dinner had mostly been prepared by his maid the day before; in addition, he'd picked up a few things at a rotisserie.

"I'm sorry I'm such a terrible cook," he said.

"It doesn't matter," I replied, as if I were an old friend. "What's important is spending time together."

The wine had loosened my tongue. I don't remember what we started talking about, but I do remember a precise sensation. I felt brilliant and sure of myself. What had happened to the Rosa who'd lived up until that moment? The uncertain, drab Rosa? The Rosa with the weight on her shoulders, the invisible backpack filled with stones? It was as if a magic wand had erased the last eighteen years.

That evening, Rosa was a fascinating young woman, capable of entertaining two intelligent older men without ever boring them. Rosa was an undiscovered mine, even to herself. A little digging was all that was necessary to reveal hidden treasures.

When dinner was nearly over, Aldo asked me, "What would you be willing to do in order to make a lot of money?"

I gave a loud laugh. "That depends on how much."

"Let's say a million dollars."

"For a million dollars I'd do anything at all."

"Including killing someone?"

I didn't answer right away. I saw my aunt standing in front of me, striking me with the poker. All things considered, killing could be a kind of pleasure. What harm would come to the world if someone like her should disappear? Even my uncle would be happy about that.

"Yes, including killing someone."

Just then the telephone rang, but Aldo didn't answer it.

Now it was Franco's turn to question me. "And what wouldn't you do for any price?"

To gain time, I wiped my mouth with my napkin, I emptied my wineglass, I patted my lips with the napkin again. Then I said, "I wouldn't give up my ideas. Ideas don't have a price."

Franco and Aldo insisted on clearing the table without my help. "It's not right for the guest of honor to work," they said. "Have a seat in the living room until we're finished."

My legs were almost too shaky to support me, and I fell onto the sofa like deadweight. I could hear my friends' voices coming from the kitchen. They were cheerful, they were laughing.

As for me, however, I was overcome by a great sadness. I was thinking about the parrot that lived in the bar in my aunt and uncle's village. He was green, and he stayed on a perch near the television set. Drunks were his habitual companions. The more questions they asked him, the louder he screamed. They all laughed at his quips, and then he'd flap his wings for joy. Later, when the bar was closed, he'd thrust his head under his wing, all alone and mangy, and drop off to sleep in the neon light.

What was the sadness that I felt? The sadness of the farm? The sadness of the boarding school? The sadness of my mama who wasn't anywhere anymore? My eyes were becoming dangerously moist. I threw my head back, the way you do when you put in eyedrops, and I was surprised to see myself reflected on the ceiling.

It was just one big mirror up there.

As soon as they came back, I asked, "What's that for?"

"For seeing the dust better!" Franco answered.

Aldo laughed. "Don't pay attention to him. The mirror helps me keep track of my things and make sure people aren't carrying them off. I have so many valuable books here, along with various small objects.

When people see something beautiful, they all feel tempted. . . ."

As he spoke, he took a few cigarette papers and began to mix tobacco and something dark on top of a large illustrated book. Franco sat down next to me and put his arm around my neck. He was wearing very light trousers; his thigh adhered perfectly to mine.

"A fine party, don't you think?"

"Wonderful," I replied, but by now the parrot was all I could think about. After a while, at least he got a chance to be alone. What had become of the Rosa who'd been here a little while ago? I couldn't find her anymore. Now there was only the Rosa who felt like crying.

When they passed me the cigarette, I drew on it greedily. Aldo sat down on the other side of me. My head started whirling fast. It was no longer tears that were trying to get out, it was vomit. I felt my dinner rolling between my stomach and my throat, as though I were on a small boat in high seas.

Whose soft, damp hand was that? Whose voice was that? It seemed to come from very far away. What was it saying? Why were they bringing up my mother? I opened my hand and found I was holding a banknote. I clutched it tight, like a handle I might be able to hold on to. Was I sitting up, or lying flat? I wasn't in a position to say. Something heavy was crushing me, I tried to push it off, but my arms had no strength. So I did what you do when you meet a bear. I played dead.

Some time before this, Annalisa and I had seen a documentary film about training dogs. In the beginning, the dogs ran around, happy and disobedient. By the end of the course, all the joy had gone out of them; following orders was the only thing they lived for. "Get up! Sit! Lie down! Fetch! Drop it! Heel! Roll over!" The trainer had a strong voice, and if that wasn't enough, he used a whistle. If the whistle proved ineffective, he resorted to electric shock. The dogs had electrodes in their collars, and the victim would flinch and squirm, crying out in pain.

EIGHT

T HAT NIGHT and the following one I had the same dream. I'm in a big, empty house, a house full of corridors and rooms. Despite the fact that there are various tools and other items lying around— some bricks, a trowel, a paintbrush in a glass of colored water—the place seems to have been abandoned for some time. The floorboards squeak, and spiderwebs hang on the walls and the jambs. Why am I here? I wonder, but I don't know the answer. So I go forward. I advance slowly, cautiously, feeling my way along. I don't know which way to go, but it's clear that I'm looking for the way out. And just as I'm descending some stairs, I hear a child's voice. He's not playing or laughing, he's crying. "What's going on?" I shout into the emptiness of the house. "Somebody find him! Somebody help him!" All at once I realize that a fire has broken out in here somewhere. The walls are made of wood, and already the smoke is running along the corridors. The child's voice grows more and more desperate. Instead of taking shelter, I go running to find him. I climb up one floor, I climb up another, I reach the roof, and then I turn and rush down to the basement. There aren't dozens of doors anymore, there are hundreds, and all of them are closed. The sounds of weeping shift from one room to another. The flames follow me like a pack of dogs. Then the weeping becomes louder, more distinct, and I understand that someone in one of the nearby rooms is hurting the child. I'm facing three doors, and a voice says to me, "You may open only one. Choose, but do it fast." I decide to try the one on the left, I reach out my hand to open it, and only then do I notice that I have tentacles instead of limbs. Not strong tentacles like an octopus, but soft, slippery tentacles like a jellyfish. I nevertheless thrust them toward the doorknob, but they're like overcooked spaghetti; they wrap themselves around it briefly, then slide off. The heat in the corridor is almost unbearable, and jellyfish can't take high temperatures. I feel the tentacles of my legs already starting to buckle. I'm going to melt to death, I think, and I discover a man standing over me. Is he perhaps the one who pulled me out of the water? Or has he come here to help me? Now I'm flat on the floor and the child is crying louder and louder. I want to stop my ears, but I have no ears. I look at the man and see that he has two dark eyes and he's holding a harpoon in his hand. He lifts the harpoon and hurls it at me. I feel the point pass through me, nailing me to the floor. An instant before I die, I realize that the child's voice is mine.

When I woke up the next day, the house was empty. Franco came home early in the afternoon.

As soon as he saw me, he asked, "What kind of face is that?"

"I've got a headache."

"That's what happens when you mix wines."

He gave me a pill, and shortly afterward he went out again. I stayed home all afternoon and into the evening. At some point I called up Signora Giulia.

When she heard my voice, she said, "Is something wrong?"

"I've got a terrible headache."

"You must be feeling stress on account of your exam."

After the telephone call, I took the vodka out of the refrigerator and drank it as if it were water. I sat on the sofa and watched television until I found the strength to drag myself to bed. I had been lying there for a while, half asleep, when I heard Franco's breathing. He smelled like wine and garlic. He was standing over me.

"No," I said softly.

"Why not?"

"I'm tired."

"But I'm not, and that's what's important."

Who said that stars fall only on August nights? Lying there with my eyes open, I saw an extremely bright one streak across the sky. What do I wish? I asked myself. But it was too late, the star had already disappeared.

Two nights later, Aldo came over for dinner. I could have tried to escape, but instead I stayed. Where could I have found a place to hide?

I'd started drinking when it was still early in the afternoon. By dinnertime, I could barely stand up. All I remember is that we laughed a lot. At one point I heard myself say, "If I'm going to do that, I want at least three times as much money."

Because I was laughing too much, my face was flooded with tears.

By the time Signora Giulia returned, it was covered with pimples; they started on my neck and went up my cheeks. In order to avoid seeing myself, I'd hung a rag over the bathroom mirror.

"You're too emotional," she scolded me affectionately. "This exam's not worth getting yourself so worked up. After all, it's going to be child's play for you."

So that I could study in peace, she kept Annalisa with her all day long. I sat in my room, surrounded by open books, and drank vodka. Afterward I brushed my teeth and ate chocolate mints so no one would notice.

To avoid being alone with Franco, I accompanied Signora Giulia everywhere. Whenever the occasional silences that fell between us grew too long, I immediately started talking. I was afraid that the truth might come out of her mouth, that she might say, all of a sudden, "What has happened between you and my husband?"

However, at the moment she didn't seem to suspect anything, she continued to treat me as affectionately as usual. Maybe it would have been best to open my heart to her and tell her what had taken place. But then I would surely have lost her, too, and I didn't have the strength to bear that.

One evening Franco blocked my way as I climbed the stairs. I'd gone down to the kitchen to get a bottle of wine. They had company for dinner, and everyone was eating out on the terrace. He pressed me against the wall with great force; I felt the contrast between his hard body and my frailty. My eyes were level with his lips. I saw them moving as he whispered, "Don't you want to have some more fun?"

"Move or I'll scream."

Like all the other students, I left home on the first day of July with a dictionary under my arm, on my way to take the written portion of the final exam. As I was going down the stairs, Signora Giulia stuck her head out the door and shouted, "Good luck!"

"Thanks!" I called back from the landing.

I sat at a desk, staring at the blank page in front of me, and then I filled it from top to bottom with the same sentence: "I don't know what to write. I don't know what to write. I don't know what to write. . . ." When every single line was full, I got up, turned in my work, and left the classroom. It was early, so I took a little walk around the city before returning home.

As for the second part of the exam—mathematics—I didn't even go. I left the apartment and caught the bus in good time, but then I transferred to another one so I wouldn't run the risk of being seen. After eating breakfast in a bar, I walked through the surrounding neighborhood. As I strolled along a secluded street, a car pulled up alongside me. The driver was a big man with a squashed nose.

"Where are you going all alone?" he said, leaning his head out the open window.

"I don't know where I'm going," I said angrily. "But in the meantime, *you* can go to hell."

The man cursed and drove away fast, making his tires squeal.

I felt swollen. I was nervous. My period was a week late. That's because of the exam, I told myself, but this explanation failed to convince me.

In the second week of July, Signora Giulia and Annalisa went back to the beach. This time Franco went with them. The oral part of my examination was scheduled for that week.

The morning of my oral exam, I stayed home and gave myself a pregnancy test.

It was positive.

That afternoon I called up Aldo. "I know you're alone," he said. "Shall I come over and keep you company?"

Without replying, I slammed down the telephone.

And now what? Something was growing inside me, as once I had grown inside my mother.

I thought nostalgically about the twilight world of the boarding school, that world where everything had its proper place. It's impossible to go back, I thought. At the end of every tunnel, there's always a light. But if the tunnel's just a wedge, at the end there's only a deeper darkness.

I was standing there, groping, and now I knew that the darkness wasn't merely apparent. I could shove it, I could kick it, I could shout magic words, but I wouldn't be able to open so much as a chink. Perhaps I had chosen, right from the beginning, the fate of the rat that goes the wrong way—down instead of up—and collides with a stone wall.

Was there anyone who could help me?

I would never have given my aunt and uncle such satisfaction. I could just hear Turkey Neck triumphantly repeating, "I always said you were like your mother. The only thing you know how to do . . ."

My sole remaining possibility was to call the mother superior. But what words could I find to tell her that I was going to have a baby and I didn't know who its father was?

I passed a part of the three following days drinking, and another part weeping on the various sofas in the house. At last I made up my mind and dialed the number of the boarding school. Hadn't she said that she'd accept anything I told her, no matter what?

"The mother superior isn't in," the receptionist said.

"When can I reach her?" I asked, disguising my voice so I wouldn't be recognized.

"She's been in the hospital for two months. She's very ill."

End of communication.

While waiting for Franco to return, I started taking very hot baths and striking myself violently in the stomach. There was a kind of spider in there, and it was growing. Day after day, it extended its hairy legs farther. First it would invade my bladder, then my intestines. From there it would ascend to my stomach and colonize my liver. I'd feel it reaching up into my throat. Maybe it wasn't a spider anymore, but a bat, a creature of the night. Like all things that live in darkness, it didn't need eyes. It was congenitally blind, its eye sockets completely empty. That was why I was doing everything I could to prevent it from coming into the world.

They came back to town Sunday evening.

While Signora Giulia was unpacking the suitcases, I went to Franco and said, "I'm pregnant."

For a moment he remained motionless, staring into my eyes.

"Are you sure?"

"Yes."

"Don't worry, it's just a little mishap. The person who caused the damage will fix it."

The next day, Signora Giulia asked me, "So how did you do? Did you pass?"

"Yes," I replied. "I got a ninety-six."

She insisted on celebrating that evening. She bought

an ice-cream cake and a bottle of sparkling wine. When we all toasted one another, I burst into tears.

"Why is she crying?" Annalisa asked in her stupid voice. Franco was looking out the window. Signora Giulia put her arms around me.

"Rosa's crying because she's too sensitive."

The following week, Franco made an appointment for me with a friend of his, a doctor who worked in a clinic. "You'll see, it's less serious than getting a tooth pulled."

I couldn't get a wink of sleep anymore. The mansard room was like an oven in summer. Even with the dormer window wide open, I still couldn't breathe. I took one shower after another. My breasts and my belly had started to swell. "A little more weight looks good on you," Signora Giulia observed.

In the silence of the night, I looked at the stars. The sky was big, after all, so there might well be Someone up there. All alone with that thing that was growing inside me, I found that I felt like praying again. Once I'd thought that only the weak and the stupid need Him. Now I saw that I was right. I'd been stupid, and now I was weak, and therefore I was calling out in a loud voice for Someone to show His face at the threshold of the universe. Since no one else is helping me, *You* help me!

I was ashamed of my thoughts, of my hypocrisy. I was treating Him as though he were an insurance company. After the things I'd said and done, what words could I use to invoke His aid? Any supplication whatsoever would come hurtling back from heaven like a tennis ball bouncing off a wall.

Maybe Father Firmato was right, and I was indeed a daughter of Satan. Maybe the best solution would actually have been for my aunt to kill me with her own hands that night. She thought she smelled the odor of sulfur, and she wasn't mistaken. With whom had my mother conceived me? And with whom had I conceived my child?

I looked at the sky, and I couldn't weep. I looked at the sky, and I couldn't weep.

I don't know why, but a word formed itself on my lips. A word I'd never spoken. Pardon.

One night I had a dream. There wasn't a spider in my womb anymore, but a small point of light. Instead of remaining still, it was whirling upon itself, casting its beams into the darkness. I'd never seen a light so bright, so intense and transparent.

The following morning I woke up with a strange noise in my ears. Standing under the shower, I thought the problem must be low blood pressure. That afternoon, the noise was still there. It wasn't the usual whistling; it seemed more like the sound of the ocean that you hear when you listen to a seashell or to waves breaking on a beach.

I had only two days to go before my appointment in the clinic. What was I supposed to do with this child I didn't want? How could I accept someone with Aldo's face, with Franco's face? I would hate it, I would try to destroy it from the very first day. Instead of milk, I'd give it poison to drink.

Perhaps my mother had harbored the same feelings about me, had thought about dropping me down the toilet, but she hadn't done so. Now here I was, regretting her refusal to act. My entire life was a mistake. It would have been better, much better, if I had never been born.

The morning of the operation, Franco gave me cab fare for my return trip from the clinic, which was practically outside the city. I left the apartment well in advance of my appointment so that I'd be sure to arrive in time. When the bus dropped me off in front of the building, I was an hour early.

I had no desire to go in and wait, so I walked around for a while. I saw a few recently built villas, some fallow fields, four or five barns, and, nearly overwhelmed among the barns, a little church. It must have been put up when the city was still far away. The air was already scorching. The door of the church was half open. Thinking of the coolness inside, I pushed the door and went in. It was tiny and not at all pretty. The floor was tiled like the floors in a dentist's office.

An ugly crucifix towered above the altar. Instead of looking dead, the figure of Christ seemed to be writhing in agony. He was all twisted and distorted, as though the pain was still devouring his bones. By contrast, the flowers in the two vases below him had already died. They leaned, wilted and drooping, out of dirty water.

On the right side of the altar was a statue of the Virgin. She was wearing a crown of little lights, like a gondola, and a long blue and white cloak. She had her arms flung wide, as though waiting for someone to welcome. Her feet were bare, but this condition did not deter her from crushing a serpent's head with her naked heel.

Two burning candles were trembling in front of her.

They're about to go out, I thought, and just then some sparrows came rushing in through a broken window. Twittering loudly, they pursued one another through the air as if they were playing. After flying around for a while, making quite a racket, they perched on the two arms of the cross.

They weren't playmates, they were a mother and her young. Now the little ones were peeping and flapping their wings as the mother fed them, sticking her beak down their tiny open throats. They asked, and she gave. She was feeding them, even though they were already fledged, even though they were already big enough to fly on their own.

The Virgin, gently smiling, continued to look at me. There were two pinkish spots on her face, one in the middle of each cheek, just above her cheekbones.

I lifted my eyes to her and said, "Aren't you supposed to be the mother of us all?" Then I reached out my hand and touched the foot that was crushing the serpent. I thought it would be cold, but it was warm.

A half hour later, I was on the examination table in the clinic. The doctor, Franco's friend, was applying the gel for the ultrasound. The noise of the ocean was still in my ears, like waves pounding and receding.

"Doctor," I asked him, "is it possible that I can already feel my child's heart beating?"

He laughed aloud. "What an imagination!" Pointing to a spot on the screen, he said, "At the moment, what you call your child is not much different from a globule of spit." Then he added, "Get dressed and have a seat in the waiting room. We'll do the procedure in half an hour."

I put my clothes back on and started to wait. After some time had passed as I sat there, I smelled my mother's scent. The combined smell of her skin and her cologne water. A scent that I hadn't smelled for years. The smell of the shower of kisses. I looked around. There was no one else in the room, and the windows were closed. Then I understood, and I did the only thing I could do. I got up and left.

There was a telephone booth next to the bus stop. I called up Franco at his office.

"How are you?" he asked me.

"I'm fine, because I've decided to keep it."

"Have you lost your mind?"

"Maybe."

"You want to bring another poor, unhappy creature into the world?"

"Maybe."

There was a long silence, and then he said, "I would never have expected such foolish behavior from you. However, you're free to ruin your own life. We'll have to see whether I want to ruin mine, too."

My belly wasn't showing yet, but it wouldn't be long before it did. What would I do when that time came?

I was mulling over this question a few days later when I walked into the kitchen and found the two of them confronting me with pale, set faces.

"What's happened?" I asked weakly, prepared for the worst.

Giulia's voice was shaking. "How could you do this to me?"

I lowered my eyes. Was this how he chose to take his revenge?

"It's true, I should have told you before."

"Told me what? That you're a thief? And to think I treated you like a daughter! I've been looking for my emerald ring for days, and where do you think I found it? At the back of one of your drawers! How many other things have vanished since you came here?"

"We made the mistake of trusting her," Franco added, fixing me with an opaque stare. "But when the root is rotten, sooner or later the whole plant rots. All the same, we were very fond of you, so we won't be calling the police. I must ask you, however, to leave the apartment by tomorrow morning. And, obviously, to give us back everything that doesn't belong to you."

My umpteenth sleepless night. Instead of resting, I passed the time thinking about the best way to avenge myself. The absence of light encourages the most terrible thoughts.

I would have liked to take his little girl and smother her with a pillow, push her into a canal, see her golden locks floating on the water like old rags. I would have liked to take a can of gasoline and empty it on his parquet floors and his wooden furniture and then drop a few lighted matches and make him die the way Indian women die on their husbands' funeral pyres. I would have liked to disconnect the brakes in his car and watch him crash into a wall. I would have liked to spit in his face, then stick a knife in his stomach. I would have liked to split him open from head to belly like a tuna and rip out his warm bowels with my bare hands. I would have liked to make him drink a deadly potion, a slow, slow poison that would cause him unbearable agony.

Then I thought that death was a gift, all things considered, and that it would be much better to have him stay alive in torment and humiliation. He could fall down the stairs and rupture his spine and have to spend the rest of his days lying on his back, with a respirator stopping his mouth. Or maybe one of the houses he'd built could collapse. Several people would die in the crash, and he'd have to go to prison and lose everything. When he got out, his wife wouldn't be there waiting for him anymore, and his daughter, a grown-up by then, would pretend not to know him. And so he'd wind up in the street, a tramp wandering from one soup kitchen to the next carrying a couple of plastic bags.

I could have told his wife that I hadn't stolen a thing in her house. I was filled with hatred, true, but that hatred had no connection with greed. I could have given her a detailed account of the truth behind my so-called theft. I could have revealed to her what her husband was really doing when he was working late in his studio. I could have told her that the child growing inside me was probably Annalisa's brother or sister and therefore, in a way, we were about to become related.

I could have told her all that, but she could have declined to believe me. Or rather she would certainly not believe me, because I was just a girl without a family, a prostitute's daughter who stole things and liked booze, while the accused was her husband. The man who maintained her in affluence and with whom she had brought into the world a daughter who was the light of her eyes. Remaining silent was less awful than not being believed.

Shortly before dawn, I took my gym bag from the armoire and stuffed into it the few things I had brought with me when I arrived.

Before I left, I slipped a note into Signora Giulia's purse. I'd written, "Someday you'll understand. Pardon me," and signed my name.

It was the beginning of August, and the city was deserted. A municipal street-cleaning truck drove slowly down the street, spraying the sidewalks and gutters with water. Dozens of martins screeched amid the roofs of the buildings. A cat with a little red collar crossed the street. I couldn't think where to go, so I walked to the park nearby. It was the coolest place I knew. There were

93

a few old people walking their dogs and a few younger ones availing themselves of the mild morning temperature and jogging.

I sat down on a secluded bench. Not far away was a little cast-iron fountain where some pigeons were perching. They took turns stretching their necks toward the spout. I could see their craws fill up and the water run down into their throats.

Farther off, an old woman with her feet wrapped in plastic bags was examining the contents of a trash bin. She was sniffing things and throwing them back. Her face looked serene, almost amused. Perhaps she'd been an important person once, she'd borne children and men had fallen in love with her.

I had often wondered what love was, but never what life was. We come into the world, each of us the very epitome of precariousness. A slightly aggressive virus, a light blow to the back of the neck suffice to send us skidding over to the other side.

We're the epitome of precariousness and an invitation to evil, to do evil reciprocally to one another. We've accepted that invitation from the first day of creation. We've accepted it out of obedience, out of passion, out of laziness, out of inattention. I kill you so I can live. I kill you so I can possess. I kill you so I can be free of you. I kill you because I love power. I kill you because you're not worth anything. I kill you because I want revenge. I kill you because killing gives me pleasure. I kill you because you bother me. I kill you because I recall that I can be killed, too.

Everything in the world has its opposite. North and south. High and low. Heat and cold. Male and female. Light and darkness. Good and evil. But if that's really the case, why is it possible to say, "I kill you," and not possible to say, "I give you back your life"? Life was born before man, and no human is capable of creating life by the power of his will. We can shout "Die!" but not "Live!" Why? What's hidden in this mystery?

While I was thinking about these things, a dog came up to me. He looked pretty old. His coat had tufts of whitish fur, his belly was swollen by malnutrition, an opaque veil covered his eyes. With an effort, he sat down near me. His mouth was open, and he was breathing noisily.

"I haven't got anything to eat," I told him, but he stayed there all the same.

The sun was starting to beat down hard, so I moved to a spot under a large chestnut tree. Its foliage provided a soft shade; swarms of insects were buzzing under its leaves.

The dog followed me. There was no bench, so I sat on the ground. He stretched himself out beside me. His breathing sounded like a bellows.

"You want me to pet you?" I asked him, placing my hand on his head. He half closed his eyes with what looked like an expression of happiness.

The sky above us was as blue as the bottom of an enameled cup. There were no more house martins, just a few pigeons flying around heavily. Higher up, the silver belly of an airplane was shining like a herring. Then it disappeared, leaving behind a white stripe, long and straight as a country road.

I wondered, are there paths in heaven? Where do they lead? And who marks them out?

Just at that moment, the dog gave me his paw.

"Is there Someone guiding us, or are we alone?" I asked him.

His eyes were nearly closed, his tongue was hanging down. He seemed to be smiling.

"Rispondimi," I said. "Answer me."

HELL DOES NOT EXIST

ONE

I'VE COME BACK to my parents' house, that house you detested for so long. I had trouble opening the door; the cylinder in the lock was rusted, and the wood was swollen from years of rain.

When it finally yielded, I had the impression that I had walked into a museum. Or into a mortuary chamber. Everything was in its place. The air was cool and damp, with that cool dampness that preserves things no longer alive from the ravages of time. The tablecloth was still on the table in the kitchen. On top of it was a pitcher and a glass. There were still some ashes in the fireplace. My mother's thick eyeglasses had been placed on the arm of the easy chair, next to a ball of wool with two knitting needles stuck into it. Our wedding photograph adorned the television set. We're coming out of the church, arm in arm, you in your morning coat and me in my long white dress. Someone must have thrown some rice at that moment, because you're smiling and so am I. But I'm smiling with my eyes closed.

My mother was the one who chose that photograph.

Many of the others were better. I pointed them out to her several times, but she wouldn't change her mind. "I want that one," she said, pointing at it with one of her crooked, arthritic fingers. I persisted: "Isn't this one better? Or this one?" "No, no, I want that one." "But why that particular one?" "Because that's the one where you're really yourself." I cleaned the glass with my sleeve. Spiders had anchored their webs to the corners of the frame.

Back then, I wondered what made that photograph so different from the others. I wondered, but I never came up with an answer. Now, in the silence of the house, I knew what the answer was. I was myself because my eyes were closed. I couldn't see, but all the same I was walking down the steps, trusting in your arm. With you guiding me, I had no doubt that I was safe.

"You see only what you want to see," my father told me shortly before he died. It was dusk, and he was standing in front of the stable. Two months later, he was dead. One night the dog came home alone. They found my father at dawn the next day, lying on his back in the moss. Animals had already started gnawing at his ears.

It was early September. We were sailing toward the northern coast of Brittany. "Your father has died," you told me as you emerged from below deck. "The funeral will be tomorrow or the day after. You won't be able to get there in time."

My mother, on the other hand, passed away while we were in Singapore on one of your business trips. No one in town knew where I was, and so no one could tell me what had happened. I found out when we returned.

When I got to the cemetery, the grass was already growing on the turned soil. It was May, and the ravines in the mountains were still filled with snow. The streams, swollen with water, bounded down amid the rocks. The branches of the larches were already covered with soft, bright green needles, the same luminous green as the meadows. At the time, I wasn't able to feel any great emotion. Maybe I was still anesthetized by your presence. Rather than living, I was watching myself live.

Then, fortunately, you died too.

When I found you stretched out on the bathroom floor that morning, it wasn't very different from seeing an insect.

Back when we were still engaged, you'd had me read Kafka's "Metamorphosis," a story you enthusiastically admired. You always said, "This work contains the whole essence of modern man." To humor you, I pretended to be enthusiastic about it, too. "It gives me the shivers," I told you. This was only partially a lie, because I actually did feel shivers. But they were shivers of disgust.

In the moment when I saw you lying there naked, with your legs spread wide apart, when I saw the soft flabbiness that the years had put on you changing into rigidity, that's who I thought of: Gregor Samsa himself. I didn't touch you, but I'm sure that if I had, I would have felt under my foot not flesh but the chitinous carapace of a cockroach.

The following week was the hardest. I had to assume

the tragic face of the grief-stricken widow. You had been an important person, and everyone wanted to offer me his condolences. Whenever all those seemly phrases became too much for me, I withdrew to the bathroom, and do you know what I did? I burst out laughing. I laughed until the tears came down, I laughed with the blithe impropriety of an adolescent. I laughed like a person who's won the lottery and can't tell anyone about his good fortune.

The obituary dedicated to you in the local newspaper filled two columns. Toward the end of it, the author wrote, "He leaves his wife and a daughter." Not a word about the son. When a person dies, his whole past becomes good. For those who must still keep on going, dragging behind them the weight of memory, isn't that the ultimate insult?

When the farce was finally over, I had only one thought: what a merry widow's life I was going to lead. You'd left me a comfortable bank account, and the curiosity and interests of my youth were still intact. I'd enjoy traveling and learning languages, I'd enroll in a watercolor class, in a literary society. I would brook no more constraints. I had to make up for lost time, so that I could be certain of dying with the serene countenance of one who has no regrets.

How could I have been so naive? Evil has many faces, it's skilled in camouflage, it insinuates itself everywhere. It may seem to have died, but it's always reborn. Although your heart had given way, your spirit was still alive. Your vengeful spirit, your destructive spirit, your spirit of hatred for everything that was able to escape your regimen of humiliation.

At the age of fifty-five, one can no longer subscribe to the illusion that her life lies only in front of her, that she can enjoy it as though she's just been born. There's been a time before which led up to this moment, and it's that time before which indicates the direction of the days to come.

When I held in my hand my mother's knitting, her thick, old-lady's eyeglasses, covered with dust, I understood one thing. Fleeing armies usually destroy the bridges they've passed over. You did the same with my life: with meticulous obsessiveness, you destroyed everything in my past. Then, to avoid the possibility that I might be able to lift up my head again someday, you undermined everything in my future, too.

This abandoned house and I are now the same thing. Dampness has eaten away parts of the walls; when it rains, water seeps in at various points. The woodpeckers have turned the shutters into sieves, while the mice have gnawed everything that it was possible to gnaw: electric wires, reserve candles, the Bible on the bedside table, the old newspapers saved for lighting fires, the dusting cloths and the pillowcases neatly placed in the chest by the front door.

Depression overcame me the very first evening. I wandered from one room to another, wearing my overcoat and carrying a candle. Everything was in such a state of deterioration that it seemed impossible to remedy the situation in a few days' time and with no one to help me. To brave the first nights, I'd brought a sleeping bag the children used to use. I went into my mother and father's bedroom, but I didn't have the courage to stretch out on their bed. Mama had been found in there, lying facedown on the floor with one arm forward and the other back, as though she were swimming.

"Did she die right away?" I asked the district medical officer.

"Who can say?" he replied, shrugging his shoulders. "I could reassure you by saying yes, she lost consciousness after three minutes, but what sense would that make? The time the dying live through is much different from ours. What seems to us like an instant is an eternity to them."

Now that I'm alone in the house, that very eternity is making me afraid. If she didn't die right away, what can she have thought in her last moments? Maybe she tried to reach the telephone, and that's why she was lying with her arm thrown out in front of her. Maybe she thought about calling me, but she couldn't make it. Or maybe she was convinced that it would be perfectly futile.

When was the last time I came to see her? She was a recent widow, so it must have been two years ago. How far was their house from ours? Three and a half hours by car, four if there was traffic.

While the children were little, I brought them here for a month every summer and a couple of weeks during the winter. The old sleigh my father had built was still there, and we'd all climb into it to go to the shops.

When we braked, the snow flew in our faces and made us all look like puppets.

Then the children grew up. Laura started wanting to be like all the others—vacations in the snow at her grandparents' place were no longer enough for her. She wanted skiing classes and chairlifts and discotheques to go to in the evenings. Not Michele; Michele was always different. He loved the house in the mountains. From the time when he was very little, a tiny child with a bright, round head, he followed his grandfather everywhere. When Michele was five years old, my father carved a little flute for him out of a reed. I used to hear those notes piping up, all of a sudden, from the most improbable places. They became extremely tiresome, those notes, but they must have seemed wonderful to Michele, for he played them over and over again. Sometimes I'd find him sitting on a bale of hay or in the stairwell. His brow was furrowed; he appeared to be thinking about something very serious.

You never liked his eyes.

"They're not blue," you used to say. "And they're not green, either. He's got eyes the color of muddle."

His eyelids and eyebrows irritated you; you found them too dark, too pronounced. "They look like they're painted on," you'd say, pointing at him as though he were an animal for sale in the public square.

When he was seven and eight, you often told him, "You remind me of that little sissy Bambi."

Then, in his adolescence, when his body grew too fast and lost its grace, your favorite refrain was, "With that painted face of yours, you look just like a hooker."

Shortly before I came up here, I heard a priest on television say that hell doesn't exist. I was busy with something else and didn't pay close attention, but a few days later I read the same assertion in the pages of one of the big national newspapers.

Hell does not exist, the article said, and this statement was corroborated by the views of a very well-known theologian. Or even if it exists, it is nonetheless empty. I was alone in the house, and I started walking from one room to another, shaking the newspaper in my fist. "Cowards! Liars!" I shouted. "In that case, where's Hitler? And Stalin? Are they strumming harps in the celestial choir? Or maybe brushing the cherubim's curls? If hell's empty, I hope they let me in at least. Ah, to be in peace down there, warmed by the flames, all alone, like a guest at a big hotel in the off season!"

After I calmed down, I thought: there you are, they're scraping the bottom of the barrel. Nobody's listening to them, nobody's following them. In their efforts to be popular, they've removed the last limit. Do what you like, perpetrate any nefariousness whatsoever, it's open house at the heavenly banquet. Joy, love, and eternity for all. Seated one next to the other, the missionary doctor and the child rapist. What a lovely party!

If hell doesn't exist, nothing exists. And hell must not only exist, it must also be completely cut off from the upper regions. There must be barbed-wire fences and flames and spires of broken glass and high-voltage electric wires and watertight compartments and a void without atmosphere or pressure and the maelstrom of a black hole that swallows all who try to escape from it. My mother and father wouldn't be able to stand being in the same place as you; they should be exempted even from imagining that you still exist somewhere in the universe. And therefore it's imperative that there should be all those barriers between what's above and what's below.

I spent the first night in the little attic room, right under the roof, in the bed that had been mine when I was a girl. Not that I slept, rather I assumed a supine position and waited for the dawn. I never lost consciousness, not even for a moment. The house was full of life. I recognized some of the noises—the mice scurrying across the floors, the weasels and stone martens turning over roof tiles in their search for a nesting place, the wood of the furniture emitting little pops and creaks as it expanded and contracted. At some point during the night, the wind began to blow. It came from the mountains, I knew, because it struck the north side of the house. The clinking of some metal rings outside, like shrouds banging against the mast of a sailboat, reached my ears. I heard the kitchen window suddenly open. I didn't go downstairs, but all the same I saw the gust enter the house and knock things over. The ball of wool rolled off the chair, and the pages of the newspapers collected for the fire started flying around the room. The small curtain drawn across the storage space under the sink began to flap, and the souvenir gondola on the mantelpiece next to the clock jerked and wobbled. All at once everything had taken on a life of its own, including the photograph of my grandmother on the dresser, complete with the sound of her voice, saying, "Anyone who dies alone remains on earth, looking for company and pacing back and forth like an animal in a cage."

After the squall died down, I thought I heard footsteps. Whose footsteps were they? They made a sound like slippers on an old person's feet.

TWO

THE HOTEL where we met isn't there anymore. The former owners are dead; their only heir was a nephew in Australia, and he never had any interest in taking the place over. The sign, or rather a part of the sign, is still there at the intersection with the main road. What's left of it reads, "The ld ot n." The Old Boot Inn.

You had come there to accompany your sister, who was recovering from a lung disease. Both of you had been there all summer, and you were bored to death. Every now and then some packages would arrive for you on the eleven o'clock bus. They contained books, and when it rained you'd spend the time in your room, reading. When the weather was fine, you did the same thing outdoors, seated on a bench or reclining on the lawn.

I could not have failed to notice you. I was in my last year of teachers' training school, and during the summer I made a little extra money by helping out in the hotel. You seemed different from all the boys I knew. At the mid-August festival, I'd danced with a corporal in the

Alpine division, but he had left me completely un-moved. The only boy in our class was the laughingstock of all the girls, including me. But when I met your eyes, I found myself blushing for no reason at all.

I was convinced that you'd never notice my existence. Then, as I was walking past the squeaking swing one evening, you invited me to join you in it. You spoke to me for a long time on a variety of subjects, like a person who feels very much alone. You didn't just have conver-sations, you conducted philosophical lucubrations; as an aspiring schoolteacher, I thought my education required me to try to keep up with you.

At our first meeting, I was grateful for your attention. By the third, gratitude had turned into pride. You con-tinued to address me formally, as though I were an im-portant person.

After a week, you lifted my hair from my shoulders and murmured, "Blue eyes and black hair, rosy lips and skin as white as newly fallen snow. Has anyone ever told you that you're very beautiful?"

No, no one had ever told me that.

Similarly, no one had ever spoken to me as you did some days later, when you were bidding me farewell, just before you boarded the bus: "Are you going to spend the rest of your life here, teaching four or five goitrous children?"

By way of answering, I produced some confused mumbles.

"My dear girl, haven't you ever thought that you could get much more out of life?"

"What do you mean, 'more'?"

By now you were standing on the top step, the folding doors were about to close.

"I mean everything! If you wished, you could have everything!"

The following summer, you returned for a few weeks, without your sister. We took long walks, hand in hand. We were always looking for secluded, romantic spots, far away from prying eyes. We'd sit under the big willow near the stream or in a clearing deep in the larch grove. And there, instead of trying to kiss me the way the other boys did, you'd take a book from your pocket and read me some poems.

With you by my side, I learned to consider myself different. I learned to understand more, to think more deeply. I was grateful to you for having bestowed on me the boldness of your intelligence.

In the end, that boldness made me restless, too. The life I'd always led was no longer enough for me. And the one that was opening out before me, down there in the valley, now seemed like a variation on a prison sentence, life without parole.

In September of that year we became engaged, and in September of the following year we got married.

My father didn't like you. My mother, for her part, did her best to defend you. "What has that poor boy ever done to you? You don't approve of him just because he comes from the city!"

At such times Daddy would hunch his shoulders and shrink a bit. "It's not that," he'd say, nervously whittling a small piece of wood. "Then what is it?" she'd insist. He'd mutter, "I don't know, I just don't like him," and become even smaller.

By the day of our wedding, I'd already learned to feel ashamed of them. The reception was held on the grounds of your parents' villa. Big tents had been put up to shelter the laden tables. Waiters circulated everywhere, carrying trays in their white-gloved hands. And wandering in the midst of all this were my mother and father, looking as lost as extras who've shown up on the set of the wrong film.

When it was time to cut the cake, my father raised his hand, as though asking for a little silence. Instead of making a speech, however, he pulled his old mouth organ out of his jacket pocket and started to play a very sad song. At that moment, I felt my hatred for him become a real, genuine physical force. After a few minutes of this torture, I hissed, "Daddy, that's enough!" But he didn't listen to me, he kept on playing for what seemed like an interminable length of time.

One of the wedding guests sighed; another barely managed to suppress a laugh. Then that laugh exploded noisily, because your father's hunting dogs arrived and began to accompany the harmonica with their howling.

Honeymoon in Vienna: first dinner, where a gypsy violinist played exclusively for us, and then the bedroom.

During our engagement, we had kissed only once, our lips barely touching. I had been moved by your delicacy.

You closed the door of the room and seized me by the wrists. Your motionless pupils seemed like a deep well that had been closed up for years.

"Do you know what marriage is?" you asked, tightening your grip.

I wanted to say, "It's loving each other," but instead I murmured, "Let me go, you're hurting me."

"Marriage is a contract. Now and forever, you're my property."

Who was this man I'd married?

THREE

IOPENED THE WINDOWS to let the dampness out. In the storeroom behind the stable, there was a great deal of cut firewood. The pannier was still solid, so I filled it and made a few trips to the house.

Only old people had remained in the village. Some greeted me, others pretended not to see me.

The church has been abandoned for years. Only on August 15, the Feast of the Assumption, a priest comes up from the valley, opens the church, celebrates mass, gets back in his little runabout, and leaves before the dampness can penetrate his bones.

Weeds are starting to take over the cemetery; parents are dying, and their children have moved to the city or even gone abroad. A single visit in November is sufficient to salve the conscience, but not enough to curb the vigor of the vegetation.

Luigi sat next to me in our one-room schoolhouse all through elementary school. After you and I had been married for years, I came upon him in the city, working behind the counter in a post office not far from our house. It was May. We had a lot to tell each other, so we went for a cup of coffee.

As you drove past the café, you saw us sitting together.

You wouldn't let me sleep for the next several nights. You kept shouting, "Who was he? You've never smiled at *me* like that!" and throwing everything you could get your hands on. Then you locked the living room doors and deafened yourself with your Mahler records.

I was already pregnant with Michele, but I hadn't yet told you.

With the passage of the years, I had come to know you, and by now I was like a trained meteorologist with a knack for forecasting hurricanes. I could almost always tell when they were about to strike and what form they would take. As a rule, I took every precaution to avoid the most violent storms.

But even the most expert scientists make mistakes sometimes. I thought you'd calm down when I said, "I'm going to have another baby." You gave me a long, long look. Then you hissed, "Oh, are you? And whose is it?" and punched me right in the stomach.

Naturally, nobody suspected the truth about our marriage. In public, on social occasions, you were an exemplary husband, gallant, generous, smitten with the beauty of your wife. When other people were present, you looked at me with starry eyes, saying, "Isn't she a jewel?"

When we were alone in the house and you needed something, you called me "Snow White." After you found out I was pregnant with Michele, "Snow White" became "Snow Slut."

You were in the Far East on a business trip the day my pains started. I left Laura with the baby-sitter and got to the hospital in a taxi. The labor was extremely long. When I saw the chief physician come rushing into the room, I knew that something was going wrong.

"What's it doing?" he asked, feeling my stomach. "What is it doing?" Alarm was in his voice. "It's turned around," one of the assistants replied. "The cord must be wrapped around its neck."

At the last minute, Michele had decided not to be born. He offered life his feet instead of his head. He tried to strangle himself with the cord that bound us. When they pulled him out, he was on the point of death.

They placed him—soft, purple, limp as a rag—on the table. A nurse said, "He's not going to make it." While the doctor was trying to find his heartbeat, Michele emitted a kind of sigh, and his little thorax began to move.

It's difficult to imagine what it means for a woman to have a child, because every child is absolutely different. For some women it can mean joy, for others only despair.

At that point in my life, I was certain that if Michele had been born dead I would have died shortly afterward. Just as surely as children represent the natural extension of the relationship in happy marriages, so too, in unions torn apart by adversity, a child becomes a sort of lifeline to be grasped and fiercely clung to, a small, defenseless thing that needs to be cared for and, in exchange for such care, daily replaces all the love that's been taken away.

True, I already had Laura, but Laura was a girl, and the older she got, the more she resembled you. Profoundly stubborn, abnormally nice when there was something she wanted, prone to sudden outbursts of rage, Laura was the apple of your eye. Even before Michele was born, I knew he'd never get that kind of treatment.

He stayed in the incubator for almost a month. When at last they brought him to me, I had the feeling that I was holding a rag doll in my arms. He lay there, rolling his watery eyes toward the ceiling, without any tension in his body, without demonstrating any will to move. While taking his milk, he often stopped distractedly, almost as though he were prey to some ancient weariness.

After eight days, you arrived. A great bouquet of red roses preceded you into the room. When we were alone, you drew the chair to the side of the bed and took one of my hands in both of yours. "I'm sorry," you said. "The child will never be normal." The doctors had revealed to you what they had kept hidden from me. "It's his brain," you added. "It was deprived of oxygen for too long."

"And so?" I cried out.

You shrugged your shoulders. "So nothing. We'll have another one."

That was the day when I realized that there's a little tiger living inside every mother. When Michele was three months old, I took him to a famous neurologist in Milan. He examined the baby at length, touching him cautiously and turning him this way and that, as though he were a poisonous mushroom whose degree of toxicity was as yet unknown.

Then we sat down across from one another. He took off his glasses and said to me, "I don't like to delude people. It would surely be more convenient to do so, but it would also be more unjust. So I'll tell you the truth. Your child will never be able to do anything. He's almost certainly deaf, and his vision is only minimal."

"Can you tell me anything more?"

"A plant. If you nourish it, it grows, it reaches for the light, but you can't ask it to speak or jump."

For the first time, I put myself in opposition to your will. You wanted to close him up in some kind of asylum and go there only at Christmas to give him a few pats on the head. I wanted to keep him with me, the way kangaroos, koalas, opossum mamas do. I talked to him all the time, stroked him, sniffed his warm skin like a puppy. All the while, you and I were arguing savagely.

The day you called him "the little bastard," I put a few things in a suitcase and went back to my parents' house. They didn't know anything about his medical history and treated him like a normal child.

It was here that he smiled for the first time. When his grandmother sang him a nursery rhyme, he burst out laughing.

You came to pick me up the following week. You

were carrying flowers in one hand and a shopping bag from a jewelry store in the other. You spoke to my mother and wept like a broken man. "Sometimes I'm a little nervous," you told her. "But I don't deserve this. Besides, Laura can't sleep anymore, she has nightmares, all she does is ask for Mama."

That night, when my mother and I were alone, she gave me a talk. "From time to time, in every marriage, one runs up against some enormously high stone steps. You look at them, and you think you'll never manage to climb them. You must nevertheless find the strength to do so, for your own sake, for your children's sake, and for the sake of the commitment you made. And later, when you're as old as I am, you'll look back, and you won't see steps anymore but meadows filled with flowers."

We left together the next day. Michele in the back, in his little baby seat, and you and I in front; we waved good-bye to my parents with big smiles and open hands. I was still young; I wanted my mother to be right.

FOUR

ONCE I READ a story somewhere. It was about a monkey and a scorpion. The monkey comes to the bank of a great river and decides to swim across it. He's barely put his foot into the water when he hears a little voice calling him. Looking around, he sees a scorpion a short distance away. "Please," the scorpion says, "would you be so kind as to give me a ride across the river?" The monkey looks him straight in the eye. "Not a chance. With that stinger of yours, you could attack me while I'm swimming and cause me to drown." "Why would I do that?" the scorpion replies. "If you drown, I'll die too. What sense would that make?" The monkey thinks about it for a while, and then he says, "Can you swear to me that you won't do it?" "I swear I won't!" So the scorpion climbs up onto the monkey's head, and the monkey starts swimming toward the opposite bank. When they're just about halfway there, he feels a sudden, stabbing pain in his neck. The scorpion has stung him. "Why did you do it?" the monkey screams. "Now we're both going to die!" "Pardon me," replies the scorpion. "I couldn't help myself. It's my nature."

What was your nature?

I tried to understand it for many years. At first I thought the cause might be some type of traumatic condition, some latent mental anguish that drove you to behave as you did. I was convinced that time and dedication would enable me to mitigate your suffering, and that one day we'd be a family as banally normal as the ones we saw in advertisements.

Then, as the years passed, my strength began to fail; I used the little I had left to defend myself and gave up trying to understand. By that time, I knew that every word, every gesture was a minefield. One adjective too many, one misplaced adverb, and the storm would break. I was cautious, I watched my step, I moved slowly, deliberately, like one who knows that there's a seriously ill person in the house and doesn't want to make any noise. The children had also learned to move in the same fashion. They seemed like two lemurs who check the soundness of a branch before launching themselves into midair.

For weeks after your death, I had the impression that I wasn't alone in the house. I'd be sitting on a sofa or walking through a room, and suddenly I'd feel a draft of chilly air. Even though it was the middle of summer, I had to put on a woolen sweater.

One night, shortly before I went to sleep, I was certain that I saw a shadow cross the space between the bathroom and the bed, just as you had done for so many years. The next day I started sleeping at a friend's house.

"Even in hell they don't want him," I told her, with a glass of whiskey in my hand.

I no longer needed to defend myself. You weren't there anymore.

Slowly, my desire to understand returned. Forty years of your life passed before my eyes, forty years in which I had come to know, or to think I knew, your most intimate depths, your every breath. Throughout those years, you'd always been able to astound me with your talent for mystification, your unchanging capacity for cruelty, for underhandedness, your constancy in feeling no emotion except the joy of inflicting humiliation on others, your taste for destroying them at the very core of their being. You resembled not so much a human being as a divinity of destruction—Shiva, for example—or a jellyfish with powerful tentacles. You spread poison around yourself, and ink. Poison, so you could kill. Ink, so you could cover your traces, so you could enjoy in secret the desperation you left in your wake.

You were a successful man. You carried on the business you inherited from your father in a way that few others would have been able to match. Your employees held you in high regard; among your closest collaborators, you were a legend. At times I even had to defend myself from the envy of the other wives—they would have done anything to have a husband like you. You never betrayed appearances. At lunch, you signed an important contract with your American partners; at dinnertime, if I didn't hurry to open the door for you, you shouted, "Where's the Alpine cow?"

For my birthday, the last one we celebrated together, you gave me a pendant with a large black pearl.

"Now we're practically old," you said. Then you lifted your wineglass and wished to propose a toast: "To your death, which I hope will be more horrible than mine."

I didn't know it yet, but your stinger had already struck me, injecting into my body the poison you wanted to get rid of.

By the time he was four or five years old, Michele was a child like any other. The results of his developmental tests revealed that he wasn't even a day behind where he should have been. The only remaining traces of his neonatal suffering were the frailty of his build and a certain inclination toward peace and quiet. Perhaps some hint from you had prompted the drastic responses of his doctors.

At that age, he openly adored you as much as you subtly detested him. The love you don't receive is the love you want the most. In the evening, around the time when you usually came home, he'd station himself by the door to wait for you. Whether you arrived ten minutes later or an hour later made no difference to him; he remained at his post for as long as it took. On the nights when you stayed out until after dinner, I had to use all my diplomacy to distract him from his futile vigil.

One day he positively insisted on my buying him a little necktie. It had been a long time since ties were in style for children, and finding one for Michele proved quite difficult. In the end, it fairly sprang out of a drawer in an old haberdashery. It was blue with red diagonal stripes. A small white rubber band served to hold the tie in place. Happiness shone out of Michele's eyes. At home, dressed like a little man, he stood motionless in front of the mirror, looking at himself and asking me, "How many buttons on his jacket does Daddy keep buttoned, one or three?"

He wanted to be completely identical to the object of his love. Until that time I'd succeeded in protecting his fragility. I did everything possible to avoid irritating you, to avoid provoking one of your outbursts of rage. If something nevertheless happened, I closed the doors and turned the radio on at high volume. I fooled myself into believing I was preserving his love for you, and I hoped that his sincere devotion would, in time, induce you to change your feelings toward him.

But you didn't notice him, didn't notice how tense he was. Or if you did notice, it was with a sense of annoyance. As far as you were concerned, the neurologist's conclusions were still valid. Michele was a retard, one who was not fit to live. And even worse than that, in your morbid imagination he was also a child who carried no trace of your genetic patrimony.

Your notions of education were very different from mine. I had studied the Montessori method in school, while your formative books had been written by Darwin and Hobbes.

"Life is a great force," you often said. "And that force manifests itself in two ways: sex and struggle." Without the subjection of the weak by the strong, without the diffusion of genetic patrimonies, life, you maintained, would have become extinct shortly after its appearance. The fact that individuals differ in their innate ability to impose their will on others was the confirmation of the principle: there were those who came into the world to dominate, and those who were born to be dominated. If you wanted to see a demonstration of this, all you had to do was consider apes and monkeys. In every group there's a male whom the rest acknowledge as the strongest, the leader, and he possesses all the females. The other males never lay a finger on the females; moreover, when these males pass close to the leader, as a sign of their manifest submission they offer him their behinds.

"How about us—how are we different from them?" This was a frequent question of yours when you were in the mood for calm philosophizing. We know how to talk, you said, we know how to make use of objects and build machines, and that's all. In the deepest part of us, in our desires, in our feelings, we're identical to them. Either you fuck or you get fucked.

What madness it was to ask you to understand Michele's delicate sensitivity! In your eyes he was just a little monkey incapable of launching himself from one vine to the next. Since you hadn't been able to fling him down from the tree—as simian groups do with defective individuals—you simply waited for him to try a vine and lose his grip. While his mother screamed in desperation, you would fold your arms and watch him fall.

When Michele was in first grade, the scales that blinded him as far as you were concerned were torn from his eyes. His teacher had asked each child to make a drawing as a St. Joseph's Day gift for his father, and to complement it with some pretty phrase. Michele was quite excited at the thought of presenting you with his drawing. As soon as you sat down to eat, he went over to you, his eyes shining with joy, and offered the gift with both hands. The page was covered with irregular, pastel-colored splotches that blended harmoniously into one another. Under the drawing, in pencil and capital letters, was written: "HURRAY FOR DADDY!"

"Well, thank you," you said as you took it from him. You turned it around and around so you could look at it from every angle.

"What is it? A cottage, a landscape? It doesn't make sense. It just looks like a big mess."

You put the drawing on the table and began eating with your usual appetite. Michele went to his place and sat down with the spaghetti in front of him and two little tears running down his cheek. After you'd emptied your plate, you noticed that his was still full.

"Eat!" you yelled at him. "Can't you see how puny you are already?"

He looked down and shook his head.

You repeated "Eat" three or four times. At the fifth, you got up roughly, knocking over your glass; the red wine covered most of the drawing. You picked up a fork with one hand and gripped his neck with the other.

Gasping for air, the child opened his mouth, and you took the opportunity to shovel some spaghetti down his throat.

After that day, he stopped waiting at the door for you. Instead of asking me when you were coming home, he ran and hid himself as soon as he heard your footsteps. The weaker and more fearful you found him, the more your animosity toward him grew. "An ectoplasm!" you shouted. "I have to keep an ectoplasm in my house!" When your paths crossed, you'd say to him, "Aren't you ashamed? You walk just like a girl."

Once Laura tried to defend him. "What's wrong with walking like a girl?"

"I forbid you to interfere!" you yelled at her, striking the door with your fist.

Poor Laura! She didn't have the extensive interior life that Michele did, but she had the same kind of insecurity. She felt suspended between a mother who was incapable of defending her and a father who was almost always screaming.

Little by little, as she grew up, your attitude toward her changed. At first she was only a stupid kid, but then she began to change into an object of a certain interest. When she was eleven or twelve years old, you often saw fit to praise her. Not for her grades or her character, but for her legs and the steadily developing curves of her buttocks. At first, your observations made her blush violently. She covered herself with oversized sweaters, like someone who's just survived a catastrophe. Eventually, however, a part of her must have understood. It was a question of living with love—no matter what kind of love it might be—or without it, of siding with the weak or with the strong.

And so at the age of thirteen or fourteen, Laura made her choice. She chose to be different from me and from her brother, and to please you. She chose to wear makeup and miniskirts at a time when her face and her body still bore the callow traces of childhood. She spoke to you the way women speak, and you treated her like a woman. At night, after dinner, the two of you would sit together in the living room, you in your easy chair and she on your lap. You'd talk to each other nonstop. Now and then I'd hear you laughing together. When you wanted to smoke, she'd light a cigarette for you. When you wanted to drink, she'd hold the glass of whiskey to your lips.

I've often come across television talk shows where older women weep over their unhappy marriages while younger women make acid comments about how weak they are. "It's your fault," the young women say. "Why don't you just forget about him?" When major crises were going on, I too said to myself, enough, I'm leaving, I'm going someplace safe! Then, when my anger passed, when my humiliation passed, I'd look around and wonder, where am I going to go? I was without a profession, I had no income, I didn't own a house that I could move into. My parents were only poor mountain peasants, and I still had two children to bring up. The law was supposed to protect me, but I knew that the law, in the majority of cases, is only appearance. It talks about the weaker and protects the stronger, the more cunning, those who have the money to pay for a better attorney.

It would have taken more courage than I had to make that sort of move. Those fifteen or sixteen years of marriage had broken me inside, had left me almost without the ability to react. Besides, I was afraid. I knew that you'd never stand for such a defeat as my leaving you, that you'd stop at nothing to be victorious again.

And so I was a virtually impotent witness to my daughter's ruin. Only once did I say, "Laura, I'd like to talk to you. . . ." She immediately turned her back on me. "I've got nothing to say to you," she answered, and she left the room before I could add anything else. By then she had chosen your world, and she couldn't betray you. She was filled with the loyalty of the favorite child.

Michele was growing too, and he grew more and more solitary, more and more thoughtful. He did well in school, but he didn't have any friends; he'd spend entire afternoons without leaving his room. He loved to read, he loved to draw. He put up with your bullying as if it were a natural occurrence, never rebelling, never even lifting his head.

Mothers often love to deceive themselves, and so I nourished a few fond hopes in regard to him. He's so absorbed in his thoughts, I told myself, that he doesn't notice how his father treats him. He didn't open up much even to me, but he was always gentle and affectionate.

Every so often, when we were alone in the house, I'd sit on his bed and ask him, "What are you thinking about?"

He invariably answered me, "Nothing in particular."

"Like what?"

"Nothing, really. Life. Death."

His drawing and painting passed through intensely passionate phases. In the first years, he liked to depict the sea or the sky; he'd take a brush and paint a whole page sky blue and then put colored spots over that. Whenever I tried to guess what a picture was supposed to be, he'd react impatiently: "Can't you see they're stars?" or "Look closely! They're all fish."

His elemental period was succeeded by his animal period. He didn't portray squirrels or sparrows; he was interested in ferocious animals. Big cats: jaguars, tigers, leopards. He'd always catch them in the instant before they pounced upon their prey. There was great concentration in those yellow-green eyes, in those coiled bodies, a concentration that would shortly explode with unspeakable force. It seemed impossible that these pictures could have been drawn by a child who was barely ten years old.

Once I asked him if I could frame one of his pictures and hang it in the living room; his reaction was terrified. "No! No!" he repeated with uncharacteristic determination, putting the sheets in a folder and closing it with a rubber band.

Then his feline phase was replaced by crosses. He made big ones and little ones, sometimes spreading them about the page in disorder, sometimes repeating them in geometrical patterns. They were all, without exception, black. In rare instances, some element of landscape surrounded them: a tree stripped of its leaves, an abandoned house deep in the country.

One day when he was in school, I gathered up all his drawings and took them to a psychologist. She examined them for a long time. She kept stroking her chin with her hand, and from time to time she asked me some questions. I cared nothing about the cats and the ocean; I wanted to know about the crosses. What did they mean? Was it normal for a twelve-year-old boy in good health to produce such drawings?

The psychologist blamed everything on the suffering he'd endured at birth. Those moments passed in suspension between life and death must have left an indelible mark on his personality, she said. The boy probably didn't realize it himself; he was just uncritically repeating religious formulas that he'd learned in the home. I objected that no one in the family was a believer, and that aside from baptism my children hadn't received any kind of religious upbringing. She seemed to hesitate. She looked at the drawings a little while longer, then hazarded a guess: "Well, maybe that's exactly what he's trying to tell you. He misses something. . . ."

A few months later, Michele reacted for the first time to one of your rages. Naturally, he did so in his own way. We were both long familiar with the escalation of your anger, we could foresee every stage along the way. So, a moment before the final scene—broken dishes or kicks to the legs—Michele folded his napkin, murmured

"Excuse me," stood up, and went away. You were petrified with astonishment. Then you looked at me and ran off to find him.

He wasn't in his room, nor in any other room. He had gone out alone. Where could he be? To deprive you of satisfaction, I pretended to be calmer than I really was, but as soon as you went into your study I hastened away in search of him. I wandered around the neighborhood all afternoon. The more I looked for him, the blacker were the thoughts that assailed me. I thought about his innocence, about his sadness, about all the risks that he might be running.

I returned home a little before dinner. The apartment was in darkness. I turned on the hall light, ready to start calling the hospitals, and I saw him crouching in a corner. He looked frail, bony; he was holding his head in his hands and sobbing. "What's happened to you, Michele?" I said, more than once. "What have they done to you?"

"Nothing," he said, without uncovering his face. "Nothing. . . ."

"Then why are you crying?"

"I'm crying for Jesus," he replied, finally looking me in the eyes. "I'm crying because He died for our sins and no one understands."

FIVE

T HERE'S A PHOTOGRAPH of Michele here on top of the credenza in the kitchen. It must have been taken at the age when he underwent his great change. He's in a meadow, helping his grandfather make hay with a scythe in his hand bigger than he is.

During that period, this house had become his safe harbor, his last refuge. He knew that with his grandparents he could be himself, that he'd find here no judgment, no contempt, just the affection of tranquil people. His vacations with my parents had never bothered you. At bottom, they were as good as any other way of getting him out of your hair. But when you realized that those holidays were happy days for him, you started to oppose them. Every time he planned to go for a visit, you'd invent some objection or tell him he was punished. Happiness was like a poison to you, you couldn't bear to see it shining in anyone else's eyes.

Unbeknownst to you or me, Michele had begun to frequent the parish church. A young priest was assigned there, and they got along very well. Upon reaching his fourteenth birthday, without saying anything to anyone at home, Michele made his Communion. I was the first to discover this, and I tried to keep it hidden as long as possible. One day, however, as you were coming home from work, you saw him entering the parish youth center.

"Since when do you go to such places?" you asked him at dinner. "Have I perhaps given you permission to do so?"

With the impromptu effrontery of adolescence, he looked you right in the eye. "I've made my Communion. Soon I'm going to be confirmed."

For a moment I feared the worst. But you remained motionless, perfectly in control of your words and your gestures.

"Ah, yes? I'm not surprised. What could I expect from a cretin like you? Go ahead and rub yourself against those pews, wear out your knees if you want. You sure aren't good for anything else."

I don't know if it was because of his age or because of his new associations, but Michele was becoming stronger. For the first time since he was born, he had friends. From time to time he went on hiking trips in the mountains or spent his afternoons collecting paper and rags. Instead of drawing, now he sang. He was old enough to have his own key to the house, and I used to hear his voice even before he opened the door. His timbre was changing. One minute he was a baritone, the next minute he sounded like two pieces of glass being ground together. His singing didn't bother me, but I was afraid it would bother you. His false notes and the words he sang would irritate you, the pure light that radiated from his eyes would irritate you. So with great prudence, pretending it was all a joke, I said to him, "Maybe you shouldn't let your father hear you singing until your tone gets better!"

By this time Michele was almost as tall as me. Standing in front of the open refrigerator, he shrugged his shoulders: "Never mind about that," he replied. "A few false notes never killed anyone."

Faced with the change in him, I realized that I too was reacting ambivalently. On the one hand, I was happy to see him opening up; on the other, I was afraid that someone might be able to take advantage of his fragility and exert undue influence over him. So every now and then I'd ask him, "Who are you seeing, what do you all do when you're together?" He always gave me some inadequate answer. If I insisted, he'd say, "If you're so interested, come along."

Once while you were on a trip abroad, I went with him to mass just to make him happy. He absolutely insisted that I should hear one of his friend's sermons. As we were walking down the street, he kept telling me, "You can't listen to him and remain indifferent. You'll see, it's like finding yourself in front of a wall. If you want to keep moving, you're forced to change direction."

We sat in one of the front pews. It had been so very many years since the last time I was inside a church that I didn't remember a single word. I didn't want to disappoint Michele, so I moved my lips, pretending to pray.

The text for the sermon was the Gospel story about the treasure hidden in a field. Michele was completely absorbed, but my brain was teeming with thoughts. I couldn't unequivocally resign myself to the change in him. The psychologist had put me on my guard—she'd said he would try to compensate in some way for his fragility. I had lived for months with the specter of drugs, of alcohol, of depression, and instead my teenager had become devout. I told myself that everyone finds his own happiness as best he can: one will root for a soccer team, another will go to church every day. Nevertheless, I couldn't rid myself of an underlying anxiety. What was it? Fear of losing him? Fear that he'd go down a road I'd be unable to comprehend? Or perhaps an unconscious form of envy, envy of his credulity, because now he lived in a universe where everything had its proper place?

I, too, during my most difficult years, had tried to cling to altars. Often, when I was passing by a church, I'd go inside and kneel down in front of a statue. But that statue always remained a statue. I'd ask, "Who are you? Speak to me. Help me," and I'd obtain no response. Had I knelt down before a stack of canned tomatoes at the supermarket, it would have been exactly the same thing. You always told me that religion wasn't much different from a baby carriage. You ride in one because you're incapable of walking on your own two legs. And when you're in a baby carriage, your movements are limited; you can go forward and backward, left and right, but you certainly can't climb stairs or go running through a meadow.

Naturally, I kept these thoughts of mine from Michele.

After we left the church, he asked me, "What did you think?" I replied in the most banal way: "Very interesting."

He occasionally told me about his meditations. I mustn't have been very good at pretending, because once he said to me, "You don't seem very enthusiastic."

"I'm glad to listen to you," I replied, "but as you know, I have my own ideas and it's difficult to change them."

He leaped to his feet, shouting angrily at me. "Why are you so blind? Jesus isn't an idea, He's the Savior. Jesus is the beginning and end of all things. He's life and the key to understanding it."

Before I could reply, he left the room.

It was the first time he'd behaved that way toward me. We'd lived together inside an affectionate cocoon for fifteen years, and now it was broken.

Around the same time, the people at his school called me up. They wanted to know why his attendance was so poor. I was simply astounded. I saw him leaving the house every morning with his book bag on his back. I'd never imagined that he could be going anywhere else.

I went back to the psychologist. She told me that a mystical infatuation was pretty normal at that age, when the hormones go into action and the libido starts behaving like the boss. When it's repressed, it can take a direction different from the customary one. Then again, she added, maybe going to church allows him to experience a latent form of homosexuality without ever letting it burst into the open. She advised me not to give the matter too much importance. If I didn't let it become a reason for opposition, it would collapse in a short time, the same way it had expanded.

I followed her advice. I kept you in the dark—I didn't want to make everything more serious—but I confronted Michele.

"Why aren't you going to school?"

"Because it bores me."

Everything came to light at the end of June, when he was failed. As you looked over his report card, your comment was, "I always told you he was a moron." Even if I'd had the courage to reply to you, in this instance I wouldn't have known what to say. Then you turned to him. "How long do you think I'm going to keep on supporting you while you do nothing?"

Michele didn't flinch from your glaring. "You can stop now, if you want."

"Oh, yes? And how do you think you'll make a living? Turning tricks?"

"I'll live like the lilies of the field."

"Don't talk bullshit."

"It's not bullshit, it's my faith."

"Your what?"

"I believe in Jesus."

You burst into loud laughter, and then all at once you stopped. In a wailing falsetto, you sang out, "I believe in Jesus! I believe in Jesus! Only a little faggot like you would fall for that drivel."

"I'm not a homosexual."

"If you were screwing like everybody else you wouldn't be getting these notions. No one with any balls is going to believe in a poor sap so incompetent he got himself killed."

"Don't blaspheme!"

"I'm not blaspheming, sweetheart, I'm telling the truth. Jesus was a mythomaniac, not to mention something of an innocent in political diplomacy. That's why he got himself killed. He overestimated himself, he got his calculations wrong."

"Jesus is the son of God."

"If he were the son of God, he'd have come down from the cross and incinerated everyone in sight, even the Bible says so. He didn't come down because he wasn't capable of coming down."

"He didn't come down because He didn't want to come down."

"He didn't come down because he was only a poor son of a bitch who told himself a pretty story. The story ended badly, and he got nailed down and hoisted up."

Michele rose to his feet. He seemed to have grown even taller than you.

"The poor son of a bitch is you!" he shouted in your face.

"Michele, that's enough!" I said, raising my voice.

But it was too late. You knocked his glasses off with one blow and slapped his head back to its proper position with another.

"What did you say?" you kept repeating, shaking him like a skinny branch. "What did you say?"

He remained silent, but he continued to look you straight in the eye.

You started yelling, "I'm in charge here! Lower your eyes!" The more you shook him, the more he withstood your glare. You dragged him to his room like that. I don't know what took place in there. I heard you shouting louder and louder. He stayed quiet.

After a time that seemed endless to me, you left his room and locked the door behind you.

"He's punished," you told me, slipping the key into your pocket. "And he's staying punished until I decide otherwise."

SIX

HOW LONG did his imprisonment last? Ten days, maybe fifteen. I had your permission to open his door three times a day. "If you try anything smart, I'll notice it."

You were fooling yourself when you chose that way of breaking him. Every day you hoped he'd beg you to let him out, but he stayed up there in his room without feeling any apparent anxiety. He read, he wrote in his diary. When you weren't home, he sang. We were still in the month of June.

Early in July you flew to Thailand to oversee your factory there. Since you had left no instructions in the matter, I let him out of his room. Laura was facing the written portions of her high school graduation exam, and I wanted to give her as much support as possible. When Michele asked if he could go to his grandparents' for the haymaking, I told him, "Go right ahead."

He wasn't my dreamy baby anymore, he was a big boy with pretty clear ideas. He demonstrated a determination that often made me feel uncomfortable.

He wrote me a letter from up there. The first and last letter of his short life. I've read it so many times I know it by heart.

Dear Mama, today I hiked all the way to the screes above Comeglians. The air was cool, and there wasn't a single cloud in the sky. Grandma didn't want to let me go, but I talked her into it. I know the paths up here better than I know the streets in our neighborhood.

Whenever I come here, I realize that all the days spent in the city are days spent holding your breath. Everything around is so ugly, so sad. If I open my nose, I smell the stink of exhaust pipes, and I hear their noise if I open my ears. If I open my heart, I see the wretchedness and solitude of the other hearts. To live far from nature means to live far from beauty. And to live far from beauty means to live far from the thought of God. I know you'll snort at this point. You think I'm like one of those cooks who put too much salt on everything.

I put God instead of salt, and you can't bear it. You think that God should stay in the churches and in the heads of priests. But do you remember? You told me so yourself: God is an idea. An idea equal to all the other ideas. I can believe in God or in Che Guevara. I can even believe in nothing but the Ferrari team victories.

This is why you feel so alone, you know. Every now and then you look around you like a lost little girl. Maybe you can fool yourself and everyone else, but you can't fool me. There's fear in your eyes, you have too many ideas in your head, and when all is said and done you don't know which of them is the right one.

But God isn't an idea! He's the place where we come from

and the place where one day we'll be reunited. He's the loving mercy that guides us on our way. Oh, Mama, how happy I'd be if you'd open your heart, if you'd let yourself rest like a newborn baby in His arms!

I always feel so powerless around you. When I try to talk to you, you grab my words with forceps and hold them up to the light for a long time, as if you're looking for something hidden. Is there a watermark? Or not? Are they real? Are they counterfeit?

You're convinced in your heart that my faith is hiding something under its apparent serenity. Some fear, some unresolved problem. Something I'm afraid of or don't want to look in the face. You may not believe me, but I can assure you that it isn't so. Since I was very little, there's been a great anxiety inside me. Maybe that's why I didn't want to spend time with other children. What anxiety? The anxiety of feeling suspended, incomplete. I could still perceive the thick darkness I'd only recently emerged from. I sensed that one day another not very different darkness would open before me. What was I doing there in the middle? It was as though I had a crystal sphere inside me like the ones that magicians have. Only mine wasn't bright; it was cloudy, opaque. My music, my painting, my always keeping to myself—those were only attempts to make that sphere brighter. I'd kneel in front of it and rub it like Aladdin rubbing his lamp. Sphere, light up! And one day the sphere lit up.

Not until then did I realize that it wasn't a sphere, all closed and sealed, but a flower bud. The rays of the sun touched it, and its petals opened. It had only been waiting for that caress before it let itself be invaded by the light.

That was the day when I understood that inside each of us there's this bud. It may be smaller or larger, its flowering may be more or less advanced, but it's there. Just let a little light filter in, and the blossom will begin to open.

For this reason, I'm taking the liberty of asking you a question: why, instead of thinking about ideas, don't you think about the Light? You don't have to defend, judge, reject, or approve anything anymore. All you have to do is relax, drop your reservations, and acknowledge that you're a child not of chaos or of chance, but of the Light.

Poor Mama! By this point you must be dying of boredom. Just think, here you are getting lectured by your own son. It's my fault—when I find something beautiful, I can't stop wanting to share it.

Guess what happened to me when I reached the slopes of the screes! I came upon a marmot nursing her young. They were hiding under a big rock. The mother didn't run when she saw me. She remained at her post, her little ones kept nursing, and she looked me right in the eyes. It was the first time I'd ever seen a marmot so close. Usually I hear the whistling sound they make and then catch a glimpse of a little shape disappearing into a burrow. You see, Daddy's wrong about this, too. He says that animals are afraid to look a superior creature in the eye, but he's wrong. Maybe it's true for baboons, but not for marmots.

After eating my lunch near a clump of mugho pine, I stretched out on the ground to look at the sky. How lovely it would be if our lives could be that limpid, that serene!

I've often thought about the recent battle. Daddy can't stand me, he's never been able to stand me, because I'm different from him and he can't figure me out. Sometimes I get exasperated, too, because I try to give as little trouble as possible, and still he *attacks me all the time. I'm starting to think that the best solution would be for me to move out of the house soon. In the meantime, I could spend the whole summer with Grandma and Grandpa. What do you say? I believe this autumn I'll have an important decision to communicate to you two, and I have to feel strong enough to do it. Even though I cause you problems in everyday life, I always pray for both of you, I pray that your buds will accept the light, sooner or later, and turn into flowers. And I thank you both with immense gratitude, because your unselfishness has given me my existence in this world.*

Here's a hug almost as tight as a python's from your unfortunately ex-docile child,

Michele

This letter arrived on the same day you came back from Thailand.

"Where's your son?" you asked me. I told you the truth: "He's gone to help his grandfather with the haymaking."

You were adamant in insisting that he should come home. "He doesn't deserve to have any kind of vacation."

I had to carry on lengthy negotiations over the telephone. Michele didn't even want to consider returning home. It was only when I said to him, in a voice close to tears, "But at least think about me, think about how your father will torment me," that he replied with a sigh, "All right, I'll come."

In the months, in the years that followed, I've never stopped thinking about that telephone call. I've heard it, heard it yet again, taken it apart, and put it back together. I've tried to imagine all the pivotal points, the exact moment when fate, instead of continuing straight ahead, shifted into reverse. But in the end, no matter how much I shuffled the cards, the response was always the same. At the bottom of everything there was one single thing: my lack of courage. I should have had more faith in Michele, I should have come forward and defended him, I should have been less afraid of your violent reactions.

It was the end of July when Michele came home. The city was already incandescent, the streets were almost deserted, and the asphalt gave underfoot. Laura had completed her high school graduation examination. She'd never been particularly brilliant in school, and she remained true to herself on this occasion as well: her grade was barely above passing. You weren't at all shocked. "A woman's treasure," you were fond of declaring, "is certainly not in her head." You generously offered to throw a big graduation party for her in the villa. Since your offices were already closed for the holidays, you were on hand to join in the celebration. Every time I passed around a tray of hors d'oeuvres, I saw you in the midst of a group of her girl friends. They were all laughing at your witticisms while you put your arms around their hips.

Michele arrived that evening. The music was at top volume, and the house was lit up like a discotheque. He immediately went up to his sister and embraced her. "So you did it, huh?" The two of them remained like that for a while, close together, without saying a word. Then she went back to dancing and he dropped down heavily into a chair.

He looked around with a smile on his face. I observed him for a while and felt a sensation of remoteness. Where was my son in that moment? Was he there, present in that room, or was he somewhere else? I couldn't tell. Soon one of Laura's girl friends came and sat on the arm of his chair. They started laughing and joking together. You dove down on him like a falcon, grabbed him by an arm, and forced him to stand up.

"Is this your party?"

"No."

"Then get out. You don't have anything to celebrate."

I was afraid of how Michele might react. But he only straightened himself and silently left the room.

I don't know why, but seeing him so docile hurt my heart. I'd have liked to follow him and talk to him, but at that moment I couldn't leave the kitchen. I thought I'd go to his room right after you fell asleep. I'd been struck by the words in his letter, they seemed like a sort of gangway thrown across the chasm, something that would allow us to refashion the sorrowful course of our two lives. I wanted to go to him and let him nestle against me, feel him go completely limp in my arms as he used to do when he was a baby. We could stay like that and talk all night long, even though now he was big enough to hold me.

But then weariness overcame me. You were still awake, going from room to room, opening and closing drawers as though you were looking for something. As for me, I couldn't keep my eyes open.

Oh, well, I thought, I'll put off until tomorrow what I wanted to do today. And I fell into my last sleep as a mother.

SEVEN

NOW I KNOW that that day was like a photographer's flash for me. I hadn't yet taken up my pose, and I was blinded by the sudden light. In that precise instant, my existence came to a standstill. The years I've lived through since were compressed into a fraction of a second.

Often, in novels or news stories, one reads about premonitions. All at once a person knows intuitively that something serious is about to happen, and then that something really does happen. I didn't notice a thing that morning. On the contrary, I woke up in an unusually good humor. The next day we were going to leave for our annual summer boat trip, sailing with some friends to Sardinia. I had to do the packing and see to various last-minute details. By paternal decree, Michele was still punished and had to stay home and water the plants. Michele seemed quite contented with this decision. Sailing had always been torture for him. He left the house shortly after you did, before the worst heat set in. Laura stayed home, sleeping late.

I hadn't seen Michele that morning, but I wasn't worried about him. He'd always had his secret comings and goings. We all had lunch together, eating the previous evening's leftovers. In the afternoon you went back to your office to put a few things in order, and I left the house to do some errands.

We didn't all meet again until dinnertime.

It was extremely hot. To make the air circulate, I'd opened all the windows. A great number of mosquitoes and gnats were whirling around the halogen lamp. Every now and then the room was pervaded by the sharp odor of a roasting insect as smoke curled up from the lamp.

As always, we had waited for you before sitting down. Taking our seats at the table before you did would have been a lack of respect that you wouldn't have tolerated. Instead of coming home at eight o'clock as you always did, you came home at eight-thirty. Your face was very drawn.

You dropped into a chair and said, "Somebody stole my money."

"What are you talking about?"

"It was in the drawer, and now it's not there anymore."

I was about to say, "Maybe some gypsies broke in," when Michele spoke: "It was me. But I didn't steal the money, I borrowed it. You weren't home, so I couldn't let you know."

You remained perfectly still. But I saw the veins in your neck pulsing at an unusually high rate.

Breaking the silence, I said, "Michele, what could you have been thinking?"

"I met a person who needed it."

When you began speaking, your voice came from deep down, it sounded almost like a rattle in your throat. "Who are you now, eh? Who are you? Are you Robin Hood? Do you rob from the rich to give to the poor?"

"I've told you I'll pay you back."

"Oh, yes? And how will you earn the money?"

"I'll work."

"You'll work. How do you suppose I earned that money?"

"Certainly not by the sweat of your brow."

Your arms began to tremble visibly. "By whose sweat, then?"

Michele remained silent, as though lost in thought. I wondered if he was afraid. I was afraid for him. He gave a deep sigh before he said, "By the sweat of the children you exploit in the Far East."

At that point, all hell broke loose.

Laura ran out of the room; I awkwardly tried to separate you and Michele. "You little slug!" you shouted as you struck him. "Thanks to them, *you* eat, too, and buy your faggot clothes, and go to school. What do you think you are? You think you're different from me? You think you're better? Answer me!"

"Different, yes. I believe in something."

I heard a weak voice, my own, saying, "That's enough! You're going to kill him!" You gave me a violent shove that sent me reeling backward.

"Oh, yes? And what do you believe in? Stealing?"

By now Michele was on the floor in a corner.

"I believe in love."

"Then go peddle your ass."

"In the love of the Spirit."

You grabbed him by his T-shirt and lifted him off the floor. Next to his slight body, you really seemed like a monster.

"In that case," you growled in his face, "turn the other cheek!"

With a childlike smile, he replied, "Here it is!"

Old-time movie projectors used to take a good deal of time to bring a scene into focus. At first, everything was confused; there were no faces or landscapes, just splotches of light and color in continuous motion. That's the way I remember the hours before the magnesium flash. I remember Michele being thrown out of the house. I remember hurling myself at you and shouting, "You're going to kill our son!" while you held on to my wrist. Inside of me there was a tigress; someone had set fire to her tail, and she'd gone mad.

"He has a noble soul!"

"I don't give a fuck about his soul!"

I don't know how long we went on this way, screaming everything we could think of at each other. I felt as though I had left my body. It could have been for minutes or maybe hours. In the end you flung me against the credenza in the front hall and left the house, slamming the door behind you.

I heard you start the car in the garage and race down the gravel driveway. You were gunning the engine the way drunken teenagers do. You slowed down for an instant in front of the automatic gate. When it opened, you took off at top speed with your tires squealing.

There was a sound of sudden braking. And then a thud.

I was afraid you'd run over a dog, so I walked out onto the balcony for a look. Stretched out on the asphalt, Michele seemed to be sleeping. He was lying with one arm flung out above his head and the other limp along his side, the way he used to lie when it was too hot in his baby bed.

EIGHT

HATRED IS THE ONLY emotion that doesn't fade away in time. In fact, with the force of a hurricane, it continues to build up, like living, potent energy. In all those years, it was hatred that kept me alive, that made me stubborn, cold, thirsty for revenge.

I could say, I live only for the memory of my son. Instead I'll be honest and say, I live only to avenge him.

Or better, I lived with that expectation.

But that expectation was thwarted the day I found you lying on the bathroom floor. I had hoped you'd have an atrocious death. Brain cancer, say, or some immuno-depressive disease that would reduce you to a skeleton in big diapers. However, with the good fortune that always protects evildoers in this world, you took the best death—a sudden, massive heart attack—for yourself and left the other one to me.

I'd hoped that returning to my parents' house would make my suffering less intense, but I hadn't reckoned with the silence, nor with the memory of the dead.

I hadn't reckoned with the oxygen in the mountain air, which nourishes the brain and heart better and makes every sentiment stronger. As in ancient times a wife was burned alive on her husband's funeral pyre, so I've collected the objects in the house that are dearest to me and put them on my bed. At night I get under the covers and feel less alone. Those objects still have life in them, they breathe, they give off heat. Even the pajamas I'm wearing aren't mine—they're Michele's.

As I was walking through the house the other night, I passed in front of a mirror and saw that I was radiating light. Was it me, or someone standing next to me? Was it the light of love, or the light of hatred? I asked softly, "Who are you?" A mouse, or maybe a dormouse, was walking on the floor above my head. "Who is it?" I repeated more loudly. One of the floorboards creaked. I had the impression that it was about to get windy outside.

Tragic fatality was what the local newspaper wrote the next day.

Michele died instantly. You got out of the car and put both hands in your hair. You hadn't seen him, you couldn't have imagined that he'd be running toward you while you were roaring out of the driveway like a lunatic.

I did nothing, I stayed there on the balcony, unmoving, as though I were in a loge at the theater. I saw the ambulance arrive and the doctor shake his head.

By the doctor's side, an old white dog appeared. I noticed him looking at you with his mouth open and his tongue out, as though he wanted to tell you something.

I saw you seize the doctor by his lapels, I heard him shout, "It's out of our hands." Then you kicked the dog. Instead of yelping and going away, he sat down stiffly on the asphalt next to the body.

I saw the police arrive, and then the hearse. First they put Michele into a plastic bag, and then into a metal container. When they slid him inside, I heard a dull thud. It must be his head, I thought, his head's been too big ever since he was a baby.

I remembered the first sweater my mother made for him, in a soft shade of blue with kittens embroidered on the front. The pattern was for a baby of six months, but it wouldn't fit over his head; she had to add two buttons to allow it to pass through. I saw the top of his bright head again, I saw that the fontanel was still open. I tried to pull the sweater on, and he protested. It was May and we were in my parents' house. He had just had his bath, heat and the fragrance of talcum powder were emanating from his body.

When the undertakers slammed the doors of their vehicle shut, the spell was broken. I screamed "Noooo!" as though it were the only word in the world. Then I lost consciousness.

All through the funeral you had your arm around me, holding me tight. I was crying, you seemed made of stone. I remember a great crowd of faces and some young people who played guitars. The August sun beat down on us.

His friend the priest was sweating under his vestments. "For a reason hidden from our little human minds, Heaven often calls its most luminous children back to itself, brusquely interrupting their earthly journey."

Two tears that he didn't bother to conceal streaked his face. "It's easy to rebel against so mighty a judgment, it's easy to be angered by it. Michele brought light into our lives, and in our selfishness all of us would have wished that this light might last longer."

His grandparents were in the front. Just before the casket was lowered, they knelt down next to it. His grandmother lightly kissed the lid. I saw her lips move, saying softly, "Ciao, bambino." His grandfather had the little flute in his hand. He left it there, with a timid caress, on the coffin.

Then there was nothing but darkness. Darkness, darkness, darkness. Darkness with bursts of light. Darkness with lightning bolts, with thunderclaps. Darkness with hail. Darkness with earthquakes and typhoons. In flashes, I saw faces, I heard voices. Your face, saying to me: "I'm going on the boat all the same." A doctor's face: "These will take care of the problem." A priest's face. "Go away!" I screamed. My mother's face: "Michele's with us still." "Stupid liar." Every now and then there were termites on my body, they reached the most intimate creases, and from there they would devour me in tiny bites. At other times they were spiders, many, many spiders, hairy and black, with short, thick legs. They ran all over me, looking for the best place to inject their poison. At still other times they were slender snakes, they wrapped themselves around my ankles, darting out their deadly tongues. When I saw my face in the mirror again, it was the face of an old woman. There are grandmothers' wrinkles and witches' wrinkles. All of mine were the wrinkles of a witch.

After the tragedy, Laura went to study abroad. She telephoned me once a month to say nothing at all.

You threw yourself entirely into your work.

"It was an accident," you kept saying. "You killed him," I replied. And this was our whole relationship.

I stayed with you so that I could hate you until the very end. But that wasn't the only reason. I stayed with you also because I wouldn't have been able to survive even for an hour alone with my grief.

How naive I was to think that I could beat you on your own ground! I've spoken of termites, of spiders, of deadly vipers, but not of scorpions. The scorpion was you.

I can still remember how indignant Laura got one evening when we were watching television. The program was a documentary about child prostitutes in the third world. Your response to her was calm, befitting a grown man of the civilized world.

"You mustn't let yourself be taken in by sentimentalism," you told her. "Their lives aren't like ours. They don't study, they don't read, they don't have anything to eat. When they're five, their uncle screws them. When they're six, they go on the street. You meet them, you look them in the eyes, and you immediately understand that they don't know how to do anything else. It's their destiny. And besides, they support their parents and their little brothers and sisters."

"You mean to say it's a good thing?"

"No, only that it's hypocritical to be too shocked by it."

Why didn't I give you a slap? Why didn't I give you one on an infinite number of other occasions? I don't know why. Or perhaps I know too well. Because I was afraid, because I was entirely in your power, and maybe because I thought you were right, after all. Because millions of people blindly followed Stalin and Hitler and all the other dictators without ever being so much as grazed by a doubt about the justice of their actions. Once you even said it to me: "I married you because I wanted to reproduce and you were beautiful and healthy. I married you because you were poor and you had no escape." You didn't say, "Because you were stupid," but you surely thought it.

Now, at the end of my days, wasted by the virus that has left me like a pile of worm-eaten timber, I understand that I could have made different decisions every day of my life. Every hour. Every minute. Every second.

It wouldn't have taken much. A little more confidence would have been enough. Raising my sights just a little higher would have been enough.

NINE

THE WIND'S been blowing for three days, and it's brought the clouds. Summer's coming to an end; the peaks of the mountains are already white with snow. As fall approaches, the smell of the earth changes. The sun no longer dries up the previous night's dampness, and the fields stay wet. The leaves of the apple trees are starting to turn yellow, the maple leaves are reddening, the needles of the larches are ablaze. Woodsheds are being filled for the winter. Any day now, the cows will come down from the mountain pastures.

They finally brought Michele up here last week. I didn't want to leave him down there in the city, next to you. A small grave beside his grandparents, near the spot that will soon be mine. I planted some marigolds from the garden there, yellow and orange, like so many little suns. Let's hope that they can hold out, that the frost will be late in coming.

I've heard it said that there are some mothers who succeed in capturing their dead children's voices on tape.

They leave the recorder on during the night, and in the morning when they play the tape back they hear loving words. Others swear they've seen their children, mingling with a crowd or suddenly shining beside them. None of this has ever happened to me. Michele has disappeared into the void, he hasn't spoken to me, I've never seen him again. Maybe I've been too skeptical. Or, once again, I've been too afraid.

The house is ready for the winter. I've replaced the windows and cleaned the chimney and the stoves. There's now an electric water heater where the old wooden one was.

The house is ready, but my heart isn't. There's more calm inside me, but no peace; sometimes my hatred rises and spills over like dough with too much yeast in it.

I don't forgive you, and I will never forgive you.

The earth isn't light under my feet; it will be even less so when it's above me. I'll become an errant soul, a ghost that goes about in chains, the first inhabitant of hell. Or the last. Or I won't become anything at all.

Everything's banging tonight. It's terrible. I hadn't remembered how much the north wind can resemble a hurricane.

I haven't slept a whole night through in twenty years. Sometimes I lie quietly in bed, sometimes I get up and walk around the house, drink some milk, listen to radio stations broadcasting from countries far away. I did something like that tonight: I got up, put on a big woolen sweater, and went to the kitchen. I couldn't stop thinking about hell, about the stupid thing I'd heard that theologian say one day. And so I took pen and paper and sat down to write a letter:

Dear friend, the theologian whose name I don't remember . . .

Suddenly the lights went out, and I had to get up and light a candle. Then I went on:

Some time ago I saw one of your programs on television and was quite offended by it. I could go along with you on one point. Hell is currently empty, because all the devils of every hierarchy are roaming about the earth. I am neither ignorant nor backward; I make my assertion only because I shared my life with one of them. Every day I look at what man has come to and I realize that he couldn't have done everything by himself. The devil isn't primitive or foul smelling. His principal endowment is his cleverness. He has a rare knowledge of the human soul, and he can worm his way into anybody at all. He doesn't employ filthy or disgusting language; his arguments are rational, refined. Years ago he said to me, "Don't you believe you deserve more from life, much more?" and I thought that he was right. I didn't have to settle for anything anymore. He doesn't show his privates and he doesn't fart; on the contrary, he escorts you into the labyrinth of life with the grace and agility of a professional waltzer.

Hell is empty only because the master of the house has gone into the world of the living to fill up his nets. Pretty soon he'll go back down, literally bent under the weight of his prey. They'll all be screaming and shouting and putting up resistance. "That was the end of the game? Why didn't anyone tell us?" But it will be too late.

Somewhere I've read that people close to God in old paint-

ings are portrayed with large ears because they are directly listening to His word. We, on the other hand, now live in a world of moles. We're blind, and our auricles are practically invisible. I've tried very many times to prick up my ears, to attune them to heavenly sounds, but unfortunately I've never heard anything coming from that direction.

On the other hand, I've always heard a mighty noise rising up from here below.

I'd like to have faith, to resolve everything before I have to go, but I can't. I've seen evil spreading in great abundance. Like an ink stain, it has invaded my life and the lives of those close to me. Injustice, inequality, violence: these and no others are the laws that govern the world. And so I say to you, please leave us, if nothing else, the joy of hell. A hell as crowded and noisy as a beach in August. I can't wait to sink inside it and suffer forever. I've caused only sorrow in my life, and so it's right that I should live in eternal sorrow.

One last thing. You also said that we should love the devil, because the devil is alone with his desperation.

Permit me to suggest to you that we don't have to give any more of a damn about the devil's tears than we do about the crocodile's.

Best wishes.

And at the bottom I scrawled my illegible signature.

It was almost five in the morning, and the sky was still dark. The electricity hadn't come back on. I took the candle and went in search of an envelope. There were various kinds in the drawer under the telephone. I pulled out a white one, and hidden under it I found an old sheet of paper, folded in half and yellowing. The handwriting was Michele's.

> *Night in the hut in the mountains. The stars are shining on the rocks and the woods. But their gaze is cold. Feeling of solitude. Where am I going? Night enlarges questions, makes them unapproachable. I start breathing again only when the soft gleam of dawn appears.*
>
> *O Lord, how great is Your mystery! To give us light, You have created darkness. To give us life, You have created death.*

As I was reading these words, a gust of wind entered violently, almost tearing off one of the windows, sending papers and ashes flying, overturning my mother's knitting basket. It held a collection of material left over from all the sweaters she made for us in the course of her life. There were the remnants of Laura's pullovers, of Michele's, of mine, of my father's. I could still distinguish them perfectly well by their colors. Pushed along by that invisible hand, they started running everywhere. I got down on my knees to try to gather them up.

The first one I grabbed was sky blue.

In that instant the candle went out, and a shaft of white light flashed across the room.

THE BURNING FOREST

ONE

I KNOW HOW OLD she is, but I don't know what she looks like. That's what keeps me awake at night. She came into the world on the third of March, at three in the morning. At three in the morning of March 3, 1983.

A friend of mine who's an expert in esoterica congratulated me at the time. Not everyone, he told me, is born with such perfect numbers. I didn't pay much attention to what he said. Giulia was slightly underweight and rather ugly, like all newborns.

She passed her first few days in an incubator. A touch of jaundice, nothing more, but it was enough to make her mother quite anxious.

"They're hiding something from me," she kept saying with a frantic look on her face. "There's something I mustn't know."

I sat on the bed and spent hours reassuring her, even though my efforts were completely useless.

When they finally laid the child in her arms, she

looked at her the way you look when you suspect you've been sold damaged goods.

"She's not nursing enough," she said. "Is she breathing or not? I don't understand what's going on."

Eventually she managed to put doubts in my mind, too. One afternoon, I accosted the head doctor of the clinic in the corridor.

"What's wrong with my daughter?"

We were standing in front of the window to the nursery. Giulia was sleeping under the lamp with her behind in the air. She was probably dreaming, because she kept making little faces.

"Why should there be anything wrong? Look at her," he said, smiling. "She's a little flower that can't wait to grow."

We went home the next day. Anna seemed calm, but the change of air hadn't done Giulia any good. She confused day and night. She screamed as though she were hungry, but as soon as Anna offered her breast the baby turned her head away. It was only after persistent efforts that her mother managed to make her take a few sucks. The struggles were exhausting, and once Giulia was back in her crib Anna often burst into tears.

"She doesn't want me!" she cried. "She doesn't want anything to do with me."

With the pediatrician's consent, we switched to bottle-feeding after a week. For Giulia, this was a decided improvement, but not for Anna. Childbirth triggered a state of depression that had been latent in her for some time. She stopped bathing, she didn't do the shopping, she didn't cook. In the evening, when I came home from work, I'd find the baby hungry, crying, and dirty from head to toe.

In a very short time, I had to learn how to be a mommy. I was changing the baby's diapers, dusting her with talcum powder, testing her milk to make sure it was the right temperature.

When I was in high school, the girls always used to tell me that I was the best of all the boys. My male schoolmates insinuated that I was gay, but it wasn't true. I liked reading better than playing soccer. If I went out with a girl, I was more inclined to talk to her than to immediately start putting my hands on her.

Maybe this was the reason why I wasn't particularly upset when I found that I had to play the mother. Instead of going to the bar and drinking with my friends, I accepted my responsibilities. It takes two to make a child, I kept telling myself. If one parent isn't well, it's only right that the other one should take up the burden. One day she'll get better, I thought, and my sacrifice will have served to build the foundations of a happy family.

I loved Anna more than anything in the world. I loved her fragility, her unpredictability. I especially loved the fact that she couldn't live without my love.

We met in high school. She showed up in my class in junior year, shortly after moving to town with her family. She sat in the third row, and she was very quiet. While the other girls were doing all they could to attract attention, she did her best to hide. Silent, soberly dressed, she blushed whenever she was called on. Naturally, she became the class laughingstock. The other girls said, either she's an idiot or she's hiding something. The boys shrugged their shoulders: forget about her, she's just a little nun, and besides she's flat as a board.

One afternoon I ran into her in the park. It was May, the swans were swimming in the little lake, stretching out their necks, and the sparrows were darting around in the dust. We spoke about our high school, about the teachers we liked and didn't like, about the graduation examination, about the holidays, about what we would do after that.

At one point I asked her, "Don't you have any passions?"

"Passions?" she repeated, lowering her eyes. "Yes, I like to read. Poetry, novels . . . that is, I'd like to major in literature. But I'm undecided, because I'd also like to study psychology. People have so much going on inside their heads. It would be great to understand something about that, don't you think?"

"Oh, sure," I replied, and then I told her about my passion for trees. I intended to major in biology or agriculture.

She looked astonished. She was probably wondering how a person could be passionate about such boring things as trees.

I told her, "Trees have personalities, too. Have you ever considered that? They can be nasty or nice. For example, look at that one. It's an Arizona cypress. What do you think about it?"

Anna stared at it for a bit, then made a face. "Nasty."

"How about that one?" I went on, pointing at a weeping willow.

"Nice. Very nice."

In that moment, I thought that this was the kind of girl I could fall in love with.

There followed the prolonged panic of preparing for the high school graduation exam, the relief of having passed it, and the brief vacation before beginning the process of registering at the university. Along the way, I lost sight of her.

We met again a few months before I got my degree. I was in the lobby of a train station when she came up to me and said, "Do you remember me?"

We went to a bar for a drink.

"How about this one?" she asked me, pointing at some leafy branches above our heads.

"It's a hackberry," I replied. "Nasty, very nasty."

The following year, we got married.

In this long period, I've written Giulia many letters. I began four years ago, first sending her a card for Christmas and then a note for her birthday. I spent a long time hesitating over the card, holding my pen suspended in midair. How was I supposed to sign? Your daddy? Your father? Saverio? Or maybe Your daddy, Saverio? I couldn't make up my mind. I unsealed and re-sealed that envelope so many times that it looked all old and worn out when I finally sent it off.

The following year, I got my courage up and sent her my first real letter. I chose some stationery that I thought would be appropriate for her, for a person of her age. It showed kittens chasing a butterfly. The letter took me more than a month to compose, it was like cutting the words into stone. Then I left it lying on the table for another month. After I mailed it, I waited eagerly for an answer. Anxiety was the sole distinguishing feature of my days: would I hear from her or not?

At last a letter came for me, but it was my own, returned to sender. The purple stamp read, "Addressee Unknown." I'd sent the Christmas and birthday cards to the same address. What had gone wrong? Maybe something had happened to her grandparents. Or maybe she herself was ill. I couldn't stop worrying. The family had lived in the same house for generations; was it possible that they would suddenly change their address? Or maybe it was just that her grandparents didn't want to give her any correspondence from me. They tossed it back into the red postbox, the way you toss a fish that's too small back into the water.

Go back. Go back where you came from.

Most of the time I watch television, especially programs for teenagers. I ask myself, which one would she like better, this one or that other one? Is she a pop music fan, or does she prefer to spend her time in the garden, looking after the plants? Is she the joy of her grandparents' hearts, or a thorn in their sides?

Often, at night, I dream about her. I find myself on the streets of a big city, New York or Los Angeles. I seem to see her in the midst of the crowd. She's walking ahead of me, I call her, but she doesn't hear me. Then I run after her, finally I touch her shoulder, she turns around, and I don't recognize her. "Excuse me," I stammer. It's a banal dream. A banal person's banal dream.

After the thing happened, they looked up some of my fellow students from high school or university days. They wanted to ask them what kind of person I was. A few of the people they talked to even had trouble remembering me.

"Saverio?" they repeated, as if they were looking for some worthless thing in the bottom of a trunk. Then they said, "Oh, yes, he was a normal guy. Extremely normal. Who would have thought it?"

I try to think about something else, but I can't. The face I remember is the one she had when she was four years old. She was losing her baby fat. Before she went off to the day-care center, Anna put two little braids in her hair. She left the house singing to herself and carrying her pink plastic lunch box. She's a part of me that's still at large in the world, still looking around, still marveling. Does she know the truth? I don't know whether she does or not, and I'm not allowed to find out. For many years I thought about disappearing from her life. For many years I thought about killing myself.

I think about Giulia, but not about Anna. Why? Because Anna is living with me again.

At some point she returned, and instead of pushing her away I welcomed her. It wasn't easy, and it took a long time. At first I didn't want to see her; then I became afraid. She spoke to me, and I couldn't believe what she was saying. I felt uncertain and confused. So I asked for an appointment with the psychologist. After I saw him, things seemed even less clear. I tried the psychiatrist next. He gave me some drugs. My tongue swelled up, and she was still here.

"Listen to me, Saverio," she would say, speaking softly, tactfully. Then I'd cry out, run around, bang into the four walls. It was as if someone had set me on fire, as if there were a tape recorder inside me, playing on and on of its own accord.

"You want to kill me, too!" I shouted at her one night when I woke up in the dark.

A powerful northwest wind was blowing. Dawn couldn't have been far away, because I heard the fishing boats returning to port. Her voice made a rustling sound.

"No," she answered. "I want you to start to live."

TWO

S EAGULLS KEEP to a regular schedule. At dawn, they fly out over the sea in little groups, bound for the mainland. A little before dusk, they travel the same route in reverse. They spend the daylight hours in one or another rubbish dump, feeding on the foulest things.

When we lived in the city, I often saw them fighting over a few morsels of garbage. They resembled chickens in a henhouse more than seagulls. What had become of those noble birds, the inspiration of poets down through the ages? These were stupid, graceless, greedy. It was impossible to imagine that they were the same majestic, impressive animals that took flight every evening at twilight to regain the open sea.

Which is the real seagull? The snow-white, solitary soarer, or the winged bully wallowing in filth?

And if that's the way it is with these unconscious creatures, how can it be with us? How can we be so arrogant as to say, look, this is me? Who am I? I don't know; at the most, I can know how I appear. How I appear to myself, how I appear to others.

For many people, this is enough. We're bit players, we ought to be satisfied.

At a certain point, however, even bit players can rebel. We can get tired of playing the same part every evening, making the same bow, speaking the same line. And so, without warning, someone or something prompts us to rip off our clothes, to roll around in excrement, to say indecent words.

Who spoke to me? Did I take orders from someone, or did I act of my own free will?

I've never believed in the soul, but I do believe in DNA. It's invisible to the naked eye, and yet it's several miles long and lasts for centuries, or rather thousands, millions of years. This fact should suffice to make any assertion of knowledge whatsoever ridiculous.

Without knowing it, one could be descended from a great-great grandfather who was a throat-cutter. Not a professional, but rather one who slit throats for the fun of it. If someone rubbed him the wrong way, he immediately jumped on the offender and opened a new smile for him under his chin. And so his distant descendant shaves every day, and when he sees a pedestrian in a crossing he slows down, stops, gestures courteously, and lets him pass. And when there's a parents' meeting at his children's school, he reconciles the bitterest differences; his reasonableness helps everyone to agree on the best solution.

But then the gene that has lain dormant for centuries suddenly wakes up, and instead of settling a quarrel the great-great-grandson slits the adversaries' throats. And then, sure enough, there are cries of wonderment and horror. How could it have happened? Who would have thought it? A person so kind, so polite.

The night passes, and it's very long. A night as interminable as the nights the sick live through. You call upon the dawn, you wait for it, and the dawn doesn't come. And then you ask yourself, where does that gene come from? Is it really necessary for evolution? Homicide among creatures of the same species is extremely rare in the animal world; among humans, it's practically the norm. You eat, you drink, you procreate, and you kill your neighbor. That's the music of every life. Therefore I ask, where does it come from? Abel was good, Cain wasn't. But in the beginning Cain seemed good, too. He plowed his soil and fed his animals, just like his brother. All at once, something happened and he wasn't the same anymore. Why?

If you can't define hatred, how can you define love? Any word you use runs the risk of sentimentalism. I can say only this. There wasn't a day, or an hour, or a minute during which my thoughts weren't concentrated on Anna. I woke up and thought about her. I drove the car and thought about her. I worked and thought about her. I thought, and I wondered, how can I help her, in what way can I make her life easier? I knew that she couldn't manage without me. Her life illuminated mine and gave it a meaning.

After Giulia's first birthday, the situation began to improve. Giulia was precocious, she had a cheerful nature, and this somehow served to reassure her mother. She'd walk down the street, pushing the baby carriage, and everyone would stop her and say, how adorable your child is, how pretty! Anna felt proud of having brought her into the world. Anxiety still consumed her, but with the help of medication she was able to keep it under control.

As the years passed, I came to know her the way a show dog knows the obstacle course. There are the three stakes, the chute's on the right, a little farther on is the wind tunnel, then the tire to jump through. Coming home five minutes late meant finding her in tears on the sofa, convinced that I'd been hit by a car. Forgetting to run an errand symbolized, in her view, the deep silence of abandonment.

When my work kept me outdoors all day long, I called her up from every bar and tobacco shop, every post office, every roadside telephone booth. When circumstances required me to bring along an assistant, I invented excuses for my constant telephoning. My mother's sick, I said, or something of the sort.

I was jealous of our reciprocal dependence. I knew that outsiders would find it a subject that cried out for uncharitable commentary. I told myself that few people have the good fortune to experience a love so intense. It was better, therefore, to keep it hidden. I listened to the tales recounted by my colleagues—ceaseless quarrels, demands for money, restless wives who waited only for the doors to close behind their husbands before rushing out of the house.

Once I myself had something of a quarrel with one

of them. He asked me, mockingly, "Don't you ever get bored with your wife?"

This question annoyed me, and I replied, "You talk like that because you don't know what love is."

I knew that our acquaintances called us "the Inseparables," but I didn't take them very seriously. That's just sour grapes, I told myself, because they'd like to be in our place.

At the time, I was employed by a company whose business was environmental protection; my specialty was diseased trees. This job afforded me the opportunity to apply my knowledge, and I was satisfied in my work.

Sometimes at night I close my eyes and I don't sleep. I see fire. It's fire, but it's not fire. It's a forest of larch trees. It seems to be fall, but the grass in the surrounding pastureland is high, and therefore it's not fall. Once again, what seems to be is not what really is. Someone's walking there under the trees, and that someone is me. The forest I'm in is the forest that's been entrusted to my care. When everything begins, it's still green. There's only the suspicion that it may be under attack from some destructive lepidopteran species. I collect a few leaves, a little bark, I strew some pheromone traps here and there to see whether the insects have already arrived.

Meanwhile, at home, Giulia has fallen out of her high chair and got herself a big bump on the head. There are no telephones in the forest, so I don't know what's happened. I find out only when I'm on the way back.

When I enter the house, Giulia's lying on the sofa, Anna's hugging her and crying.

"It's my fault, she can't see out of one eye."

The stakes, the tunnel. It's useless to reassure her, useless to tell her that all of us have fallen out of our high chairs a few times.

Early the next morning, I take them to the hospital. From there, I call my colleagues at work and tell them I'm going to be a little late. But the doctor comes out of the first aid station, and next to him is Anna, looking like a ghost. I hear the doctor say, "We'd best admit her right away."

That same day, the lepidoptera reach the forest.

Usually, a forest dies more slowly than a person. It takes months or even years for it to pass away. But once it's gone, it's gone forever, and all the other forms of life are gone with it. Lichens and moss, beetles and red ants, weevils and crossbill finches, goldfinches and titmice. Whatever can escape does so. Whatever can't make it dies with the trees.

My death and the death of the forest began with curious synchronicity.

There was something wrong with Giulia's head, but they still didn't know exactly what. They had to open it to find out. I walked on the first fallen larch needles, not worried about Giulia, but about Anna. If Giulia dies, I thought, that will mean that it was her fate to die, but how will Anna survive her? I kept walking, and suddenly

I felt her thin shoulders. How much weight was piling up on them?

As she passed her days at the hospital, Anna became more and more transparent; her voice was reduced to a bare whisper. Whenever I could, I held her tight in my arms, I spoke softly into her ear.

They had shaved Giulia's head. Now her eyes looked enormous, and the happiness was gone from them.

In those days I should have been terribly depressed, even desperate, but instead I felt like a lion. I was filled with extraordinary energy. I was the strong foundation; I couldn't give way.

The operation went well, and so did the postoperative course. Now we had to wait for the biopsy results. A few days before we got them, Anna and Giulia came home.

In the forest, the first two trees had turned yellow. Merely touching a branch was enough to send needles cascading down like rain. Needles that fall unseasonably are more disconcerting than leaves. A leaf glides down; a needle plunges. Fallen needles seem like teeth, and the bare branch is like an exposed gum. Everything around it is life, and there, where it is, is death. Or the prelude to death.

Anna had made friends with a nurse in the hospital. I often saw them intensely engaged in rapid-fire conversation.

One evening when I came home from the forest, I found the house empty. We were to learn the biopsy results the next day, and so I got worried.

I drove around all night long. I passed along the river

and crossed over the bridges again and again. It was possible that Anna had done something crazy. Something crazy from our point of view would have seemed like a normal thing to her.

In the first light of dawn, I went to the police station and reported the two of them as missing persons.

Shortly before noon, I heard her key in the lock. She was smiling, carrying Giulia in her arms. She kissed me as though she were coming back from a brief excursion and then went to the telephone.

"What are you doing?" I asked her.

"I'm calling Giulia's doctor," she replied.

"I'll do it!"

I saw her shoulders shudder. "It doesn't matter."

After a minute, the doctor came on the line and told her the results of the biopsy. Anna fell down on her knees with the receiver still in her hand.

"Dada, I wan' my doll!" Giulia shouted.

I shouted, "Well?" This frightened the child, and she burst into tears.

"Well?"

Anna was trembling. She covered her face with her hands and repeated, "God, I thank you! God, I thank you!"

In the end, I grabbed her by the shoulders. "Are you going to keep talking to God," I shouted in her face, "or will you deign to talk to your husband?"

THREE

FIRES NEVER BREAK out on the island. There's too much stone and too little vegetation. Fires don't break out, and yet the smell of burning is always in my nostrils. But what smell does fire have if there's nothing burning inside it? The fire in a forest is different from the fire that consumes a heap of old tires. The fire that burns up feathers and bones is different from the one that devours leaves.

At night I dream that the larches have turned into flames. Every larch is a solitary blaze. If I look more closely, I see that they aren't larches but persons. Or better, larches with the heads of persons. There's Anna's face, up there, and Giulia's, and even my own. We're all burning, but no one's making an outcry or cursing his fate. All that's audible is the dry crackling of the dead branches. And there I am, running around in circles on the ground below, pulling at my hair and saying, "They were insects, not flames! Why is everything burning now? I've never believed in hell!"

It was night when she came the first time. I felt something cool on my cheeks, I opened my eyes, and I saw hers shining in the darkness. There was a terrible sadness inside them. Something, someone, I don't know who or what, spoke to me in a whisper: "What have you done?"

I've never believed in hell, nor in devils, nor even in ghosts, and accordingly I've never believed in God, either. In fact, the very idea of God has always annoyed me. Why was it necessary to trot him out to explain the universe? There were the laws of physics, the laws of chemistry. Their interaction offered the possibility of explaining everything.

After Giulia's illness, Anna became another person.

She often went out with her new friend, the nurse, and returned home loaded down with packages. She started dressing with greater care, using a little makeup, wearing cheerful, colorful clothes.

One day I came home and found vases of primroses in every window. Instead of greeting her, I attacked her: "What do you think you're doing?"

"I thought you'd like them. It is spring, after all."

"Right, but these flowers ought to be outside, don't you know that? You could've told me you wanted to see them, and I would've brought you to look at them in the forest. But putting them there, surrounded by all this cement, with their little heads cut off . . . that's wrong. It turns my stomach." As I was saying this, I started snatching the primroses and throwing them on the floor.

Seagulls act the same way. When they have some dispute with one of their kind, they pull out grass with their beaks and fling it aside, as though to say, "Watch out! The next time, instead of the grass, it could be you."

Now I was calling her every half hour, and she was never home. In the evening, feigning indifference, I'd say, "I called you at four o'clock, but you weren't here." She was always serene. She'd answer, "I went out with Giulia and Silvia. We went to the park. . . ."

They often went to visit a certain monk who lived in a monastery just outside the city. When Anna talked about him, her eyes shone. "You should come and meet him," she used to say. "He's really an extraordinary man."

"As you know," I replied, "I'm not much inclined to that sort of thing. What difference does it make whether there's a God or not?"

"It makes all the difference!"

I'd never seen Anna discuss any subject so ardently.

"Think about a flower," she told me. "Seeing it as a flower is one thing. It's blue or yellow or red or lilac. It has petals and sepals, it has a pistil, an ovary, a stem. It can live in a field or it can cling to rocks. But it's another thing to see it as the realization of a dream. Someone has imagined beauty for us, and in order to realize that beauty he created flowers. Before it's anything else, a flower is a gift given to our eyes."

"Who taught you such a muddled way of reasoning?"

"Everything seems clear to me," she answered, lowering her gaze.

The next morning I heard her sing while she was fixing breakfast. I shouted at her from the bathroom, "Turn off the radio!"

What had become of my Anna? Where was the fragile creature who had dominated my thoughts for years? On some days we saw each other only in the morning and then not again until the evening. During the course of the day, we were strangers.

Since I no longer had to live with the stakes and the wind tunnel, I too had begun to have my own life. After work, I hung around for a while with my colleagues or went to a bar in the center of town for an aperitif. All the same, sometimes I'd come back home and find that the table was still not set for dinner.

One day a colleague at work said to me, "Why not open your eyes? When a woman changes, there's only one reason: some other person has entered her life. She dresses up, she puts on makeup, she sings. You're not foolish enough to believe she's doing that to go listen to some old monk?"

In the Gospel, the devil climbs to the top of a mountain and says to Jesus, "All this will be yours, if you obey me." The devil could be compared to a real estate agent, or to a woodworm. Or he's like one of those spiky grass seeds, the kind that slip in everywhere, alighting on the surface of a body and burrowing into its skin like a silent arrow. No one sees him as he makes his way, no one feels him as he digs his furrow. He knows exactly where he's going: up to the head, or down to the heart. And there he explodes.

So my colleague's words had been woodworm words. There I was, unmoving, and there they were, boring deeper and deeper into me. Why hadn't I thought about it before? Her new girl friend, her monk, her continual goings and comings. . . . It was evident that all this activity was only meant to serve as an excuse. In all the years our love had been alive, her eyes had never shone like that.

With a thread of suspicion, you can sew any kind of garment. Thus, little by little, I managed to reconstruct the sequence of events. And to bring a name and a face into focus. Who else could it be but the doctor? He had been very close to her throughout those days of fear and suspense, when Giulia's fate was in his hands. He had performed the operation in the best possible way, carefully and conscientiously.

He hadn't done this to save the child, that much was clear; he was interested in making sure that he was admired. He'd seen that desperate young mother, a prey offered to him on a silver platter. If he wanted to serve himself, all he had to do was to reach out his hand. There's nothing better than a woman who needs to be consoled, to be reassured. In fact, the pig had chosen his profession with just this sort of thing in mind! One after another, distraught mothers fell into his arms. And evidently the nurse, this Silvia person, was acting as some sort of go-between. It was her job to lure the victims into the trap. She befriended them, went out with them, and spoke exclusively about the doctor in order to increase their idolatry of him.

The phone call Anna made to him to get the biopsy results was the clincher. She picked up the receiver and dialed the number from memory. Familiarity showed in her every gesture, and she knew the number by heart. She, who was usually afraid to call the dairy store downstairs!

And what was the monk, if not a code name for some motel on the outskirts of town?

I walked in the forest and thought about nothing else. There was no one I could open my heart to, and so my thoughts and my anger intensified out of all proportion. I was speaking aloud as I walked. If anything was within reach, I gave it a kick. A cascade of dead larch needles fell on my head, on my shoulders. Only the idea of revenge gave me a kind of temporary peace. I imagined all the ways I could do them harm. As I imagined them, I heard my skull creak. I was clenching my teeth as tightly as if the uppers had fused with the lowers. I could cut words out of a newspaper and send his wife an anonymous letter, telling her everything. I could write obscene insults all over his elegant automobile. I could wait for him outside his house and teach him a lesson.

I couldn't hide my agitation from Anna anymore. At night, lying beside her, I twisted and turned in the bed.

One night I couldn't stand it any longer. When she asked me, "What's the matter? Why can't you sleep?" I answered, "You have a smell I don't recognize."

She burst out laughing. It sounded like lighthearted laughter. She said, "I've changed moisturizing creams!"

"You could come up with a better excuse than that," I hissed. Then I got up and went to sleep in the living room.

She followed me to the sofa and gave me a worried look.

"Don't touch me," I told her. "You disgust me."

She touched me all the same.

"Saverio, what's going on?"

"What's going on is that you've changed."

"That's true, but why does it make you angry?"

"Because when a woman changes, there's only one reason."

"And what is that?"

"You really want me to tell you to your face?"

"Yes."

"It's because she's in love with someone else."

Anna gave a deep sigh. "It's true. I am in love, but not with another person."

"With what, then?"

"I'm in love with life."

"Don't give me that soap opera bullshit."

"It's not bullshit. It's what I feel."

"So you hear the little birdies singing?"

"No, I've found a sense in life."

"Your life already had a sense. It was me, it was us, your family."

"That hasn't changed. It's truer than ever before."

A laugh that resembled a bark came out of my throat.

"It sure doesn't seem like it. 'Honey, I'm coming home late. Honey, look at my nice new hairdo. Smell this perfume. Look how my ass sways when I wear these new heels. Look, honey, look. Don't I really look like a whore?'"

Anna got up. I kept my back turned toward her.

"Why are you hurting me this way?"

"Because I see the truth."

"All you see are the figments of your imagination."

"Right. And since we're on the subject, how about taking me to meet your famous monk?"

"I thought you weren't interested in him."

"On the contrary, he interests me very much."

That night I fell asleep on the sofa laughing. I had her in a fix. Truth will out—could there be a proverb more valid than that?

It took her some time to organize this encounter. At last, after a week had passed, she told me, "They're expecting us at the monastery this afternoon at four."

We took Giulia to a birthday party for one of her nursery schoolmates and headed for the ring road. Anna was driving, and we made the entire trip in silence. Every now and then I had the impression that she was swallowing hard, like an animal aware of some imminent danger.

A series of ugly buildings, situated about a dozen miles from the city, constituted the monastery. The exaggerated blandness of monoculture, interrupted by a few rows of poplars not yet in leaf, surrounded the compound.

The entrance hall was cold and dreary. The brother who served as doorkeeper invited us to sit on two small, light brown, imitation-leather armchairs. When the door at the end of the hall opened and an old man appeared, Anna rose and walked toward him.

I watched them embrace; then, with a gesture of affectionate intimacy, he took one of her hands in both of his. I remained seated. Anna led him over to me and said, "This is my husband, Saverio."

The monk shook my hand and indicated that we should pass into a little room off to one side.

We sat down facing each other. I was looking at his beard, wondering whether it was real or fake, when he said, "Your wife has told me a great deal about you."

"Ah, yes? And what has she said?"

"She's quite worried."

"Why?"

"She says it's because you've changed, and she can't understand the reason for your change."

"She's the one who's changed."

The monk smiled. "That's true. In the past few months, Anna has experienced a genuine revolution."

"So why can't I change, too?"

"There are many kinds of changes."

"You mean you like hers and not mine."

"It's a question of the light that shines through the eyes."

A bell rang somewhere in one of the corridors.

I was starting to get irritated.

"Straight from the storehouse of decrepit clichés! 'The eyes are the windows of the soul,' et cetera, et cetera. Nowadays computers can think almost as well as people, and you still believe in these things. Or worse, you'd like me to believe in them."

The man stared at me with two dark, motionless eyes. I had the sensation of being an exotic animal in a cage. He was scrutinizing me, and I had no way of protecting myself. I've let him talk too much, I thought. Now it's time to cut him short and unmask him.

I abruptly rose to my feet. My chair fell over. "Why don't you stop pretending?" I shouted, louder than I would have wished.

The monk remained immobile, unblinking, staring at me as before. As I reached the door, he said, "Now I understand."

"Understand what?" I shouted in reply.

On the way back, I drove.

"He plays his part well, your friend," I said. "He's almost intimidating. Almost."

"Sometimes I have the feeling you've gone insane."

"Then we're both insane. I'm Napoleon, who are you?"

As I spoke, I stamped angrily on the accelerator. It seemed that I had to crush something under my foot.

"Saverio, I know it seems strange to you, but my life

has changed. It's changed because of something that can't be seen."

"I don't believe in things that can't be seen."

"But you believe in the laws of chemistry."

"Everything that exists is chemistry. Chemistry and physics. You, me, this car, the engine, the gasoline, the asphalt, the trees. Chemistry and physics create life."

"But who created them? Who created the laws that allow us to be here?"

"The laws have always existed."

"That's not true. God created the laws."

"Of course. And Eve ate the apple, and soon fire is going to rain down on the earth again. Isn't that right?"

"Don't make fun of me."

"I'm not making fun of you. Where's the address of that neurologist you went to after Giulia was born?"

"You talk like that because you're envious."

"And what am I supposed to be envious of? Your little fables? No, thanks. I believed in Santa Claus until I was six, and that was all."

"I believe in God, not Santa Claus."

"You wouldn't believe in him if Giulia had died."

"God will save us in any case."

"Oh, yeah? Let's see," I said, stepping harder on the accelerator.

"Slow down!" Anna shouted. "Think about our daughter!"

"God's thinking about her, isn't he? Let's see."

At that point, I turned into the oncoming lane at top speed. After a few seconds, another car appeared, heading straight for us. A fraction of a second before the impact, I swerved out of the way.

After we were back in our lane, I burst into nervous laughter.

"Well, who saved you? Who turned the steering wheel? God or me?"

Doubled over on herself, covering her face with her hands, Anna was crying. "You're a bad man," she repeated. "You're a bad man."

I made a false effort to console her. "Don't say that. I was joking."

Her tears filled me with a profound joy.

FOUR

B Y N O W the forest was almost completely consumed. There were only about thirty larches that
still seemed healthy. A close inspection, however,
sufficed to reveal that the first signs of destruction had
begun to appear on them, too. I'd been trying to solve
this problem for almost a year, and everything I'd come
up with had proved futile. There was no evidence of
mold, or fungus, or rot; my attempts to blame various
lepidopteran species had all been dead ends. I hadn't
found even a trace of any such insect. Then I considered
acid rain. In North America, near the Great Lakes, I'd
seen entire forests of conifers suffering from that. Here
in Italy, there was too much industry and too much in-
dustrial waste in the plain of the Po River, and whenever the wind reversed direction everything blew up
north and drifted into the valleys.

I'd been fairly convinced that the acid rain hypothesis
was correct, but water tests conducted in recent months
proved me wrong again. The forest was dying and I
couldn't figure out the reason why. The client who'd

commissioned this job wanted answers, and I kept hemming and hawing and changing my mind. I was putting my observations into a report, but it wasn't ready yet. Every day my suspicion that a virus was the cause of all the trouble grew stronger. But when you say "virus," you say everything and nothing. Insects have their laws; in order to combat them, you have to try to think like them and to find an enemy that will devour them. The virus, on the other hand, knows only one law: anarchy. It lives anywhere at all, wherever it pleases, according to laws all its own. It lives, but its purpose is not life, no, but the devastation and death of the organism that is its host. It has not one face, but many faces. Every time we manage to identify one, it puts on a new mask, changes the password, immediately crosses a border, and becomes a fugitive again.

I passed entire days languishing among those trees. The death of a tree is something that causes extreme uneasiness, especially in someone who's been charged with saving it. A tree dies without a word, and its trunk remains for a long time, too long, like a finger pointed at the sky. A finger that underlines your impotence. You knew all there was to know about its life cycle, and in spite of that you couldn't do a thing.

For many years now, going over those days in my mind, I've often told myself that the forest, too, made its contribution to my ruin. There was a virus in the forest, and there was another virus in my body. When the two came into contact, they succeeded in igniting a deadly mixture.

If at the time I had been taking care of a flourishing

garden, for example, maybe everything would have turned out differently. I would have arrived at the garden full of gloomy thoughts, and the garden, with its peace, with its harmony, would have made those thoughts disappear. The citrus trees in the big greenhouse would have been blooming, and the flower beds a triumph of color. Life with its song of beauty would have dispelled every shadow.

Instead, every morning I arrived to witness the death throes of the forest. I stayed there all day long, rained on by falling needles. I was losing control of my wife, and I was losing control of the larches.

When I was in the forest, I thought only about Anna, about how I would have my revenge. When I was home, on the other hand, I thought about the forest, about what the best solution might be. One day or another, I thought, I might go up there and really set it on fire.

I was grinding my teeth so hard in my sleep that Anna woke me up one night and said, "Listen! There must be a rat somewhere. . . ."

It was probably the third or fourth of May. We were already on daylight saving time, and I had stayed in the forest longer than usual. When I got home, it was a little past nine. There were no lights in any of the windows, and there was no one in the apartment. I was tired and dejected. I expected a hot meal and some sign of affection. After all, my family was the reason why I worked myself to death the whole blessed day.

My anger exploded all at once. I started kicking

everything I could and knocking things off of shelves. I grabbed our wedding picture and threw it on the floor, broke the glass and the frame, and tore the photograph into tiny little pieces the size of confetti. These I picked up, and when the front door opened I was holding them in my hand.

Anna seemed tired.

"A miserable day," she said. "I got a flat tire, and the spare tire was flat, too."

I stood before her and blew the scraps in her face. "Our marriage," I said. "Here's what's left of it."

"Why are you talking like that?"

"Why?! Why?!" I started to yell. "Why??? I work for my family all day long and I come home and I'm a single man. I don't have a wife or a daughter anymore. The poor fool, all he's good for is bringing money into the house. But the poor fool is fed up, tremendously fed up!"

Giulia hid behind Anna's legs.

"Calm down, Saverio, calm down. I told you, it was just a series of mishaps."

I felt like a coffeemaker that's been on the fire too long; the pressure was mounting and mounting and mounting some more.

"That's all you know how to say!" I shouted, and then I did something I'd never have thought myself capable of. I gave her a slap across the face.

There was a moment of silence. The telephone rang, but no one answered it. Giulia said, "Dada bad."

Anna picked her up and kissed her on the forehead.

"No. Daddy's not bad. He's just very tired. Look, let's pet him a little."

Giulia raised her little hand and hesitated. Surprise and fear were in her eyes. Anna took her hand and guided it to my cheek.

"Nice Daddy, nice Daddy."

Her fingertips were uncertain and cool on my burning face.

"I hate you," I whispered into Anna's ear before I went out the door.

I didn't have the car keys, I didn't have my wallet. It would have been too humiliating to go back and get them. Where could I spend the night, if not in the cellar?

Now I know that I was on a course, and I had arrived at the point where the cellar was the last tunnel to pass through, the last pole to go around before I reached the goal. I could have gone down the street, entered the first bar I came to, got smashed, and passed out on a bench in the park. I could have gone to a friend's house and stayed up talking like a madman until the first light of dawn. I could have done all this, but instead, like a robot, I started going down the stairs.

In the cellar, I found what I was lacking. A new bicycle, with a red bow tied to the handlebars, next to the bell, and a shopping bag from a men's store hanging down from them.

I had been right: there really was another man behind the change in Anna, a man arrogant enough to hide his bicycle in my basement. Sure, arriving by bicycle was easier than coming by car, and it left fewer traces. But why is it here? I wondered.

Maybe he'd been surprised by the rain one day, and so Anna drove him home in the car. "Let's just leave the bike in the cellar," she'd said. "My husband never sets foot in there."

While I was going mad on account of the forest, they were lying between my sheets and exchanging endearments.

Was it the doctor or not? By this point, it didn't matter at all. It was enough for me to know that I hadn't been mistaken.

Now the fire that was consuming the larches blazed up inside of me. I felt the flames licking the trunk, I heard the branches cracking an instant before they came crashing down.

It wasn't possible to sleep in the cellar. I sat down for a while. Then I saw two old dumbbells. I picked them up and started to work out. I did some chest and back exercises, ran in place for a while, switched to deep knee bends, and then did more chest exercises. I felt full of a terrible energy. The basis of all energy is some form of heat. I had to dissipate my heat to avoid exploding. Dawn was invisible in the cellar, so I consulted my watch continually. If you pressed a button, the dial would light up for a few seconds.

Five-thirty.

Six.

Six-fifteen.

Anna would take Giulia to nursery school at eight o'clock. I planned to wait for her return, go upstairs, and tell her what I thought of her behavior. And I'd go to a lawyer that very morning and start proceedings for a separation that would declare her to be at fault and give me custody of Giulia. I felt that victory was near.

Everything happened very quickly. I went upstairs at eight-thirty. A big white dog that I had never seen was hanging around the front door of the apartment.

"Get out of here!" I told him.

But he kept staring at me as though he hadn't heard anything. In one swift, rough movement, I grabbed him by the scruff of his neck and flung him down the stairs.

Anna wasn't home yet. I stood inside the front door and waited for her. I stayed like that for five or ten minutes.

When she came in and saw me, she said, "Where did you sleep? I was worried all night long." She assumed a look of feigned sadness.

"You didn't notice? I was very close."

"Very close where?"

"Under your feet."

"In the cellar?"

"In the cellar."

I enjoyed studying the expression on her face. She looked disappointed. "So you saw everything?"

"I saw everything."

I expected her to burst into tears at that point, to

throw herself at my feet and beg my forgiveness. But she smiled instead, and even her eyes were merry. She spread out her arms, saying, "Well, happy bir—"

Why did I still have one of those weights in my hand? I raised it and it came down on her head. There was a dull sound, and Anna fell to the floor like a rag.

FIVE

I NEVER FOUND OUT what happened to the forest.
I wonder what became of all the notes I took, all the
folders with detailed analyses and survey maps. In all
likelihood, the landowner gave up trying to save his
trees.

This is how things probably went. One morning, two
forest workers with chain saws arrived up there and
started sawing. That deathly sound—metal teeth attack-
ing what had once been living beings—pervaded the
valley for an entire week. Then the noise ceased, and the
brook began to gurgle again. The woodpeckers found
other bark to peck at, and the goldfinches and redpolls
fluttered in amazement over the great bare tract of land
that had once been their world.

Losing teeth, losing hair. At night that was all I
dreamed about. The dying forest and my own increas-
ingly toothless self. Toothless and bald. My teeth didn't
fall out one by one, but all together. When they hit the
floor, they made a tinkling sound like glass marbles.

The departure of my hair wasn't much different. I ran

my fingers through it and it came out in huge clumps, as though I were wearing an old wig. When that happened, I started weeping. I wept softly, in silence. In such a state, where could I go? Without teeth, without hair, I was capable of inspiring only laughter or pity. I could neither instill respect nor awaken fear anymore. I have never since wished to appear in public again.

The forest was dead, and Anna was dead, too. When I saw her lying there on the floor, I felt powerless, the way I felt with the trees. I hadn't thought it would be so easy to throw the switch. I'd barely grazed her, and she was gone.

For a few minutes I thought it was all a joke, I said to her several times, "Come on, get up. I was joking."

I brought her a glass of cold water.

Her lips didn't open, and the water ran down her neck and wet her blouse.

Could I run away? I'd certainly have a lot of time. I could take the car and head for the border at top speed. I could put her in a bag and drop her in some river.

But instead I remained seated on the floor beside her, holding her hand.

When someone knocked on the door, I went and opened it.

It was the postman. I took the telegram he handed me and said, "Please come in. I've killed my wife."

Giulia was still at nursery school.

One month later, my lawyer brought me a newspaper with her picture in it. I could tell it was her from her shoes, her apron, her little basket. There was a blur where her face should have been, but sticking out from the sides of the blur were two pigtails, each tied with a checkered bow. The photograph must have been taken on the morning of the tragedy, because only Anna knew how to tie bows like that. I could hear her crooning in the bathroom: "Here's a tail for my little mouse, here's a tail for my little piggy."

A stranger was holding Giulia's hand. She looked like a rag doll, her arms slack and her feet dragging. Had they told her anything, or had she figured it out without being told? In any case, blurring her face was pure hypocrisy. The picture had a caption: *Little Alice (not her real name), daughter of the agronomist uxoricide.*

Then one day when I was already here amid the odors and sounds of the sea, I suddenly opened my eyes and understood why the forest had died. Its end had been caused not by an insect or a canker or a virus but by mere envy. Envy, because the larches grew among or alongside silver firs, Norway spruces, and Scotch pines. In the summer these trees look so much alike that the uninitiated call them all "Christmas trees," but in the winter everything changes. The needlelike leaves of the larches fall to the ground, while the firs and spruces and pines keep their needles. And so the larches, naked and frozen, must look upon the others, all pliant and picturesquely covered with snow. People pass and say, look at those, how pretty they are, but these dead ones sure are sad.

Therefore the larches became envious. They gave themselves no peace: what do these others have that makes them better than us? If it was God who made us, why didn't he make us all equal? He gave all four of us needles and a pyramid shape. We grow to the same height, and we provide nourishment for the same kinds of animals. Our wood makes beautiful furniture. Our resinous vapors cure bronchial ills. So why do the firs and the spruces and the pines get preferred treatment?

For a couple of years now, I've been in correspondence with the monk who was Anna's friend. He was the one who started the exchange. I didn't answer him right away. In fact, when I saw his first few letters, I tore them into scraps, yelling, "What does he want from me? Don't I suffer enough?" Eventually, I wrote him a note, asking him to stop. He sent me a reply. I let a few more months pass, and then I replied in my turn. In all those years, he was the only person who contacted me.

He found my theory about the death of the forest highly amusing. He even added a commentary of his own. *The larches,* he said, *aren't envious of evergreen needles, they're envious of love. Isn't it the same way with people? Why do you think Cain killed Abel? Because he believed that Abel was more beloved than he. And why did Joseph's brothers throw him down a well? Because their father so favored him that he'd given him a sign of his preference, a coat of many colors, the same coat that would be found lying bloodstained in the sand.*

Whoever lives in love risks more than others and must often pay a very high price. In all my years of shepherding souls, I've never ceased to be amazed by this fact: in many cases, instead of opening people up, love causes them to close tight. Why? Do we perhaps imagine that love is like food, like water, like money, and fear that someone greedier than ourselves will come along and consume it before our very eyes? But love is like the air: infinite. It can't be broken up into little pieces, put in knapsacks or handbags, kept in the pantry. We can't take a slice of love, because we'll always find someone whose slice looks bigger to us.

This is the way the demon of envy ravages the world. The fear of not having enough makes me stingy, and so I grasp, I grab. The more I grasp and the more I grab, the more afraid I am of losing, of not having enough.

Do you remember our first meeting? The color of your soul was a fiery red. It wasn't wickedness that was inside of you, but confusion. The fire blazes up just at the moment when we're not paying attention. One flicks away a cigarette butt, and that cigarette butt sets a whole forest aflame.

You keep telling me that you loved Anna and you were afraid of losing her. But have you ever asked yourself whether you truly loved her? Did you ever really see the person that Anna was?

Or did you love her with a narcissistic love? You loved her love for you, you loved your ability to protect her. Did you love her fragility, her dependence?

When she became a strong, autonomous person, your feeling for her turned upside down. The moment Anna freed herself from fear, you began to fear her. This isn't a mere play on words, it's something serious and worth reflecting on.

What kind of life is a life lived in fear? It's the life of one who walks along with his eyes cast down. The life of a slave. But we're not called to a slave's fate; ours is the destiny of children, of brothers. It's the destiny of love and freedom. Because true freedom is not doing what we want, it's rather living like creatures free from fear.

I often think about the last time I spoke with your wife. Anna telephoned me the night before the tragedy. Her voice was full of anxiety.

"Saverio hit me, and now he's disappeared. He's never behaved like this before. The worst of it is that the child is starting to be afraid of him."

"Do you think he'll do something stupid?" I asked.

"I hope not," she said. There was a pause, and then she continued: "Tomorrow's his birthday. I got him the bicycle he's been wanting. I hope he likes it and calms down a little. Besides, you can't expect marriage to be nothing but blue skies all the time. Saverio lives in a cocoon, and he's afraid that someone will pull him out of it. Before, we both lived in that cocoon, but then I got out and he was left alone. It's as though he was shouting, 'Come back!' "

"And how about you? Do you want to go back?"

"Even if I wanted to, it would be impossible." Then she added, "Father, I'm finally starting to understand that saying."

"Which saying?"

"The one about the hatred of the world. Up until today, I've always wondered how it was possible for people to hate you when you live in love."

"Are you afraid?"

"I was, but now I feel serene. Anyway, isn't love also patience? I love my husband, I love our child. I know that he loves us too, that it's only a matter of time. He's in a world of illusions, and he just has to find his way out."

You see, my dear Saverio, you have had the great privilege of *descending the ladder all the way down to the bottom. I don't say this to you in mockery. One can see things much more clearly from a low point than from somewhere in the middle. You could have kept floating amid your confused feelings for the rest of your days. Some days would have been clear, others cloudy. One morning you'd have hated your wife; that night you'd have blackmailed her with love. Some couples carry on like that all their lives, without ever so much as imagining the possibility of emerging from their everyday hell.*

In your life, farce turned to tragedy. All you had to do to destroy three lives was to raise your hand in anger and bring it down on Anna's forehead. How long did the whole thing take? One second? Half a second? And in the next second, you were already weeping beside your wife's body.

Many people would write the words "The End" at this point. In contrast, I like to think that every end is really a new beginning. Of course, something is over, but "something" is never everything. What we call the end is often just a transformational phase. Since you've studied insects for such a long time, this notion must be quite clear to you. Anna's dead, and a part of Saverio is dead, too. Now the living part of Saverio must start over again.

Self-pity, self-contempt, self-hatred—all these are ways to make the sacrifice of your wife empty and futile. When the time comes, Another will judge you. Meanwhile, leave a space in your heart for mercy to act. Take up your burden of blindness, of violence, of confusion, of hatred, of bitterness, and start walking. Walk even if they tell you that it's useless, that you no longer have the right to walk. Keep walking even if you can't see the path anymore, even if the fog envelops you and your uncertain steps bring you to the edge of a precipice. As you walk, sooner or later you'll realize that life is a journey that must be accomplished, not a cocoon in which the most you can do is stretch out your legs.

Now, the great majority of people don't live, they simply wait for life to pass. In such cases, what does life become? Nothing but a box filled with amusements to drive away boredom. Then death arrives unexpectedly, and everyone shouts, "Cheating! Trickery! The rules of the game didn't say anything about this."

But death lies ahead of us from the very moment of our conception. It's there like a riddle, a perpetual query that we carry around inside us even on our happiest days.

Given that we must die, what sense is there to life? Everyone born must rediscover for himself the significance of this question. And making such a discovery doesn't mean that one becomes master of something; it means that one becomes free. Free from all those things that make up the burden on our backs, free from greed, free from envy. And free, above all, from the idea of ourselves.

A while ago I used the word "freedom," but I could just as well have said "purification." Purification of our words and our thoughts from the thing called "sin," which sounds so obsolete yet is in reality so extraordinarily alive. Sin isn't a transgression against the rules of a hierarchical order but a length of thick black cloth that we throw over ourselves. In that artificial darkness we see nothing, we hear nothing, and yet we're convinced that we understand everything.

It follows that sin is a kind of dereliction, an injury that we do to ourselves alone. Something that puts us dramatically far away from our proper condition, which is that of creatures born to live in the Light. You had before you your wife's luminous love, your daughter's trusting love, and yet not only could you not see them from under that heavy cloth you'd got yourself wrapped up in, you even mistook them for a threat.

Anna's death must serve to rip that cloth apart.

I'm an old man now. I've seen and experienced many things in my life, I've had various conceptions of the world. As the years have passed, I've realized that those conceptions, apparently so stable and well founded, were actually like the refracting mirrors in a kaleidoscope. I thought, every time, there you are, this is the world, this is what life is. One must act in this way or that. How long did such thoughts last? A puff of air was enough to shatter them; another world rose from the ruins, and then another, and then yet another.

At a certain point, I rebelled. This is all foolishness, I shouted. Existence is foolishness. I myself am a fool, and everything I've believed in is foolishness. For years, I've genuflected before the void. For years I've spoken about the void. For years, I've tried to convince those around me that the void is full, and that this fullness has a name and a significance worthy of veneration and respect. My desperation was absolute. Every morning I got out of bed and wondered, what am I going to do? Shall I continue to live, wearing my habit, spreading lies as though nothing's amiss, or shall I take direct action and put an end to my days?

It was terrible, you see.

I was hearing people's confessions, lost souls were telling me their innermost secrets, they were all expecting me to show them a way, a certainty, while I was wandering in total darkness, without the possibility of confiding my dismay to anyone. Seeking a new answer to my questions. I rotated the kaleidoscope furiously. And that's when it slipped from my hands, fell onto the floor, and broke into a thousand pieces. Suddenly I realized that up to that point all the things I'd believed in had been ideas, projections of my anxieties, of my fears. I'd wanted to comprehend the incomprehensible, I'd wanted to limit it, to give it a name and a term of development. I wanted to bring everything within the limited dimensions of my human mind.

That moment was the real start of my journey. At that moment, I was completely naked, completely defenseless, completely voiceless.

Now I get out of bed every day and go to the window, and I know that this day could be my last. I'm not afraid anymore, I no longer have a sense of the void, but I feel a sort of adolescent trepidation, like one who awaits the first encounter with the Beloved.

Every morning, a little before dawn, I stand by the window of this ugly cement building, look out, and see the deserted fields, and beyond them the dark shapes of the barns and the factories and the lights of the cars. So many people go to work at that hour! I stand there while the light prevails over the darkness.

It's a spectacle that never ceases to astonish me. There's delicacy in that moment, there's fragility, and also enormous potency. It's when the dark blot of the fields becomes grass. I see the blades, one next to the other, and the dew that covers them, and the insects that are drinking the dew. I see the sparrows alighting on the bushes. I hear their joyous, disordered chirping and the more precise chirping of the finches and the tits. I hear the sound of the automobiles, and I see the people inside them. I see their hearts the way I've seen the dew on the blades of grass, one by one, their stories, their anxieties, their uneasiness. I see their hearts and the hearts of the people close to them.

Their children, still sleeping in their beds, protected by warm blankets, their wives, already awake, and their aging parents, who have passed a sleepless night and now are listening to the radio. I see their hearts and I hear their breathing. I hear the breathing of those who are being born and the breathing of those who are passing away, like a great concerto played by the wind. It's organ music, or flute music. It rises, descends, rises. There's a continuous exchange between heaven and earth.

And that's why I brace my elbows on this ugly cement window ledge every morning and weep. I weep the way only the old can weep, softly, silently. I weep because I see love. The love that has preceded us, and the love that will welcome us. The love that, in spite of everything, accompanies each earthly journey, even the briefest, even the most tortuous, even the one that most abounds in error. I weep for love, and for all the souls that are born, live, and die sealed up like coffins.

I pray for you. I pray that one day you too, like me, may be able to look out your window.

A lengthy postscript followed his scrawled signature.

P.S. In the course of the last few months, I've seen your daughter several times. A slender, long-limbed teenager, she wears her hair in a ponytail as her mother did and has her mother's eyes, while her coloring and the shape of her hands are yours. She's a thoughtful girl, accustomed like you to meticulous reasoning. It takes a little while to notice the subtle disquiet that lurks deep inside her. The first two times I brought this up, she brusquely refused to talk about it. The third time, making an effort, she said, "My father's a murderer."

I replied, "Your father is a man who did a terrible thing, but he's not a bad man."

We were sitting side by side on a low stone wall. Her pants were frayed at the hems, and she was swinging her legs nervously back and forth. She looked into the distance and said, "People who aren't bad don't kill."

In adolescence, everything is black and white! I answered her like this: "Sometimes a person does something awful because he's weak or confused, because he's afraid. What would you do, for example, if a snake crept out of this wall right now? Even though you love animals, you'd probably kill it."

In time I was able to talk to her about the two of you, about the love that bound her parents. "When you were little, your mother was ill and your father took care of you as few other fathers would have done."

There was a blooming mallow plant growing at the base of the wall. A buzzing bee plunged into it.

"You see," I pointed out, "the bee needs the flower. But in order to exist, the flower also needs the bee. We're all bound up in an invisible embrace. Your father needs you, and you need him."

She remained silent for a long time, twisting a few strands of hair around her fingers. She kept her head turned so that I couldn't see her face. She sighed deeply two or three times—it seemed that she was trying to fight off something that was smothering her. Then, in a broken voice, she softly asked me, "But Mama, my mother, would she be contented?"

I told her, "She'd be the happiest mother in the world."

I walked over to the window with the letter in my hand. It was dusk, and the gulls were returning from the mainland. There were two adults above me. They were almost motionless, hovering on their great white wings. A younger gull was following behind them. His plumage was still dark. At regular intervals, he called them with a sort of long whistle.

The sea must have been a little choppy, because I could hear the waves breaking on the rocks. When it was agitated, I heard my blood making a similar sound; my heart pumped it up to my ears, and it descended again from my ears to my heart.

There was another letter in the monk's envelope. It was smaller and written on pink graph paper. I stood there and opened it while the sun disappeared over the horizon.

Dear Daddy . . .

A NOTE ABOUT THE AUTHOR

SUSANNA TAMARO is the author of six books for adults and four children's books translated in over forty countries with over 15 million copies sold. She lives on a farm in Umbria with dogs, horses, chickens, goats, and mules, where she cultivates her garden, does karate, and writes books.

A NOTE ABOUT THE TYPE

This book was set in a digital revival of Bembo, which was originally designed by the Bolognese type cutter Francesco Griffo (1450–1518), who worked for the celebrated Italian Renaissance printer and publisher Aldus Manutius. Manutius had commissioned Griffo to design a new typeface for the 1495 publication of a small treatise, *De Aetna,* by classicist Pietro Cardinal Bembo about his visit to Mount Etna. The typeface is named in his honor. Griffo also cut early italics, music types, and is attributed with cutting the first roman types with which we are now familiar. The modern version of Bembo was redesigned in 1929, under the supervision of the British typographer and printing historian Stanley Morison for the Monotype Corporation. Along with Garamond, Bembo is considered one of the first "old-style" typefaces. During the early sixteenth century the French type founder Claude Garamond used Bembo as his model for his own widely popular typefaces. For this reason Bembo is generally acknowledged to be the foundation and standard for old-style typefaces. Highly regarded as one of the most readable text-faces, Bembo has endured as a classic until today.